# JEAN BRASHEAR

## A FAMILY SECRET

*Silhouette*®

**SPECIAL EDITION**®

Published by Silhouette Books

**America's Publisher of Contemporary Romance**

There is nothing more important than family, whether by birth or by adoption, family of blood or of the heart.
To my mother, Diane Roberson, who has spent her life teaching me by example that love is the most important calling, and to the memory of my father, Ed Roberson, a true man of the West who knew all about living with honor.
And to Ercel and Anni Brashear, wonderful people who shared their son with me and accepted me into their family and their hearts as though I belonged from the start.
Thank you all for making my life rich with love.

 **SILHOUETTE BOOKS**

ISBN 0-373-24266-2

A FAMILY SECRET

Copyright © 1999 by Jean Brashear

Visit us at www.romance.net

**Printed in U.S.A.**

**Books by Jean Brashear**

Silhouette Special Edition

*The Bodyguard's Bride* #1206
*A Family Secret* #1266

## JEAN BRASHEAR

A fifth-generation Texan with pioneer roots, Jean Brashear hopes her forebears would be proud of her own leap into a new world. A lifelong avid reader, she decided to try writing a book when her last child was leaving the nest. The venture has led her in directions she never dreamed. She would tell you that she's had her heart in her throat more than once—but she's never felt more alive.

Her leap was rewarded with the publication of her first novel, and Jean is hard at work on future releases while pinching herself to be sure that she isn't dreaming all this. Happily married to her own hero, and the proud mother of two fascinating children, Jean is grateful for the chance to share her heartfelt belief that love has the power to change the world through her stories.

Jean loves to hear from readers. Send a SASE for reply to: P.O. Box 40012, Georgetown, TX 78628 or find her on the internet via the Harlequin/Silhouette website at http://www.romance.net.

## A FAMILY SECRET
## FAMILY TREE

Ben Gallagher m. Mary Simpson    Jack Wheeler m. Rose McCall    2nd m. Buster Caswell

Sam Gallagher m. Jenny Wallace ----------- Dalton Wheeler m. Lilah
(aka Edward Collins)

Secret Child

**Maddie Rose Collins**

Mitch Gallagher

**Boone Gallagher**

LEGEND:
----- Affair

## Chapter One

A man she'd never met had bequeathed her a house in Texas.

And then exposed her father's whole life as a lie.

On the heels of finding her business partner and lover in bed with the woman he'd deemed more proper to marry, Maddie Rose Collins thought nothing could surprise her now.

She was wrong.

Here she was in Texas after driving cross-country for three days. Halfway up the dusty road that led to the big white house on the tree-dotted hill, Maddie stopped, her heart drumming.

There it stood. A shiver ran through her. In the deepest part of her dreams, she knew this place. Never mind that she had never laid eyes on it before, had never even known it existed.

A picture of this place should be in the dictionary right beside the word *home.*

*Ah, you're a hopeless romantic, Maddie.* That had been only one of Robert's scathing indictments. She'd never been able to please Robert van Appel, and she was through trying to be someone she wasn't.

So here she was, with a house that could have stepped out of her childhood longings. It was the haven her father's wanderlust had denied them, the kind of home she'd given up hoping for many years ago.

It was two stories, white with a deep wraparound porch. Trees cast welcome shade, a lacy green over-skirt billowing on either side of the structure. Spotting a porch swing curved Maddie's lips in delight. She could already picture herself there in the heat of the day, with a cool glass of iced tea. Drops of moisture would roll down the sides of the glass, falling to her bare legs, cool and welcome.

She remembered the words. *I wronged your father, Maddie Rose, but it's too late to make it right with him, so I'm giving you the house that should have been his....*

*Thank you, Sam Gallagher,* she thought. *I need this.*

Her whole life was upside down. She had money

from dissolving the partnership in the Manhattan restaurant she and Robert had owned together. She had restaurants lined up to hire her as chef. The whole world was open to Maddie—

And she had no idea what to do next.

So Sam's bequest was a godsend. She needed time and space to think—and here she would have both. Assured by her lawyer that it was all legit, Maddie had packed her car and left New York to explore a heritage in Texas she'd never known she had.

She would put Maddie back together here, and figure out where to go next.

Just then, a plaintive cry sounded off to her left. Maddie's head jerked, seeking the source.

A calf worried at something near its feet, but Maddie couldn't see anything for the weeds growing just outside the fence. She looked toward the house, wondering why someone didn't come to help.

The calf bawled again, and the heart Robert had damned as too soft wouldn't let her linger. She opened the door and emerged, her sandals turning whiter with dust with every step.

"What's the matter, sweetheart?" she crooned.

The calf's head reared up; it took a jerky step backward but couldn't move far, bawling piteously.

A cow nearby stirred restlessly. Maddie gave her a glance, then looked back at the ugly stretch of barbwire tangled around the calf's foot.

Maddie eyed the weeds with suspicion. Snakes. Texas had snakes. She'd never been here, but everyone knew that. Maybe she'd just go to the house for help.

The calf cried out again, and Maddie saw blood well in the new gash. The baby couldn't wait. "Hold on, sweetie. Just let me find something to—" She spotted a big rock and chucked it at the weeds, listening for a rustling sound.

The calf jumped back, bawling more stridently. The cow bellowed.

*Better not try that again,* she decided, eyeing the ground between her and them. "Hello? Anyone here?" She looked around, wishing someone would notice and come to help, but there wasn't a soul in sight, and the calf was jerking around, ripping the gash deeper.

The section of weeds was sparse and only about two feet in depth. Surely she'd be okay.

Maddie took a deep breath and waded into her first taste of Texas.

Sitting in the kitchen of the place that had once been home, Boone Gallagher still expected to hear his father's booming voice, unable to imagine anything bringing Sam Gallagher down. Sam had fought land and weather and lack of money to wrangle a living from this harsh country. Boone still couldn't believe that his father was gone.

Or that it was forever too late to heal the breach between them.

A cup of coffee he didn't need steamed on the scarred maple tabletop. He'd done his homework here all those years ago, listening to his mother hum church hymns while she worked, back in those golden days when this house had still been a home. So many years gone. So much loss. Exhausted by twenty-eight hours of travel from the Pacific to Texas, memories knotted in his chest, Boone felt glued to the seat of the creaking chair.

He shouldn't drink this coffee. He should fall into bed and sleep around the clock. But he had to talk to Vondell first, had to find out if Sam had ever softened, had ever regretted what he'd done.

"You look like something the cat dragged in," Vondell drawled in a voice sandpapered by years of cigarettes. Barely five feet and topped by frizzy red curls, Sam's housekeeper had always ruled this place with equal parts of tyranny and affection. They all knew better than to tangle with Vondell, but even she hadn't been able to make Sam see what he was doing to all of them after Boone's mother had died.

"Thanks a lot."

"Go to bed, Boone. It'll all be here when you wake up."

He scrubbed both hands over his face. "Did he know it was coming, Vondell? And he still wouldn't send for me?"

For a moment, her hand hovered as if to touch his hair. "Boone, I wish—"

Vondell looked troubled, glancing away toward the window over the ancient porcelain sink. Suddenly she came to attention, her gaze caught by something outside. "Would you look at that!"

Whatever Vondell saw, Boone couldn't imagine anything on Sam's ranch that would be worth having to rise to look at right now.

Then it struck him with the force of a hammer blow that it wasn't Sam's ranch anymore. It was his ranch—his and Mitch's, that is—if he could ever find his brother and coax him to come back. Boone had found Mitch's whereabouts once, a few years ago, before leaving on the mission that had ended his military career. Mitch's trail had gone cold before Boone had gotten back on his feet. Then he'd met Helen and started down the road to disaster.

Too many years, too much pain. Boone had been fourteen, Mitch sixteen when their lives blew apart. Sam had roared out blame and hatred, lashed out in unreasoning, raging grief. It had been the beginning of the end—the day he drove Mitch away.

"Boone, she's gonna get herself hurt."

"One of the cows or a mare?"

"Neither. A woman."

*A woman?* Last he knew, Vondell was the only woman on this place. He rose and crossed to the window, the flash of reds and purples snagging his eye.

It was a woman, all right, one like he'd never seen around here. Her slip of a dress sparkled bright with gypsy flair. She had sandals on, for Pete's sake, risking chiggers and ticks. Never mind that a mama cow stamped restlessly only a few feet away from the woman who was reaching through the fence toward the cow's calf.

That woman was headed straight for trouble.

"What the—" Boone turned to Vondell. "Who is she?"

"I don't know." Vondell shrugged and frowned. "I didn't hear anyone drive up."

Boone crossed the kitchen.

"Wait, maybe—Boone, there's something I should—"

"No time now. I'll be back in a minute." He was already heading out the screen door toward the small pasture by the barns. "Wait right here."

Long strides brought him close enough to see a very shapely backside as the woman started climbing the pipe fence, heading toward the calf, oblivious to her danger.

"Get away from that calf!" he called out.

But she didn't seem to hear him over the bawling.

Boone broke into a run, as she neared the top. "Don't go near that calf!" he shouted.

She jerked around at the sound of his voice, losing her balance and tumbling inside the pasture. Boone closed the distance and vaulted the fence. He landed beside her as she scrambled to her feet, scooping her up and using his body to shield her. Half shoving, half carrying, he got her over the fence—and followed with only seconds to spare.

Roaring her outrage, the cow hit the metal, making it clang and shudder.

The woman in his arms shivered, the color draining from her face. Slender fingers clutched his biceps.

Her head just reached his chin. Over the adrenaline roaring through his system, Boone registered soft, tempting curves that felt much too good. "Are you all right?"

Eyes wide, the woman looked over at the cow now sniffing at her calf. Then she glanced sideways at Boone and did the damnedest thing.

She smiled.

Here Boone was, still trying to get his heart to slow down, and the crazy woman smiled. Her eyes twinkled, her generous lips curved as though she had no clue how close she'd come. "My first day in Texas and already an adventure."

He lost his temper.

"Damn it, lady. Don't you have a lick of sense? You don't ever get between a cow and her calf unless you're itching to get hurt." His hands tight around her slender shoulders, Boone quelled the urge to shake her.

"I was only trying to help the little one." She stiffened and stepped back. "How was I supposed to know he belonged to one of them?"

Her voice was Lauren Bacall, low and throaty. Boone couldn't quite place the accent, but it was from nowhere near Texas. Sassy…and sexy as hell, she was.

And a damn fool who could have been hurt badly.

He clenched his fists to rid them of the feel of her. "You don't climb into pens with animals you don't know. That cow weighs over a thousand pounds. She could crush you without even trying."

The woman's eyes sparked. "I called for help, but no one answered. How could I leave that poor thing to suffer? You'll have to excuse my inexperience." Her tone went frosty. "There aren't many cattle in the city."

Only one city referred to itself simply as "the city." "You're from New York." An accusation, not a question.

"Most recently. I've lived all over."

A city girl. Just like his wife, who had hated every second spent in this place. But at least his wife hadn't thrown herself into dangerous situations. Not here, anyway.

In the end, he'd still lost her, though. And the memory turned his voice sharp. This woman shouldn't be here. He wanted to know why she was.

"Who are you? What are you doing on my ranch?"

Soft gray eyes turned wary, studying him for a long moment that made Boone's spine tingle with unease. Fringed with thick dark lashes, a striking black ring around the irises, her eyes softened as if in sympathy.

"Are you Boone or Mitch?"

He stared at her.

"I'm Boone," he replied, frowning. "How do you know my name?"

She stuck out one slender hand to shake his, her eyes still soft. Too soft. Almost like an apology. "I'm Maddie Collins. Your father mentioned you in his letter."

She got a letter? Boone had only gotten a telegram, and that was only after Sam was dead and buried. He paused for a moment before closing his much-bigger hand around hers, registering the smooth skin, the firm pressure. "What letter?"

Her grip tightened slightly. "You didn't—?" Her eyes darted to the side, looking toward the house. "He didn't—?"

"Didn't what?" His stomach clenched. "Why are you here?"

The woman named Maddie swallowed, then straightened, shaking her dark brown hair back over her shoulders as if preparing herself. In the sunlight, it glowed hints of red like the sky's warning of storms to come.

Then her next words wiped all thoughts of silky dark hair and husky voices from his mind.

"Your father left the house to me."

"He *what?*" But even as he waited for her reply, he believed her, this stranger in too-bright gypsy colors who didn't belong here. He'd been crazy to hope that anything might have changed between him and his father, that Sam had regretted abandoning his sons.

"I'm sorry." She seemed sincere. "I—I thought you would already know."

Her regrets didn't matter. At that moment, he knew only one thing. He wasn't through losing things that mattered. He'd been a fool to think otherwise.

Even in death, the man who'd been barely a father

still denied him the only place he'd ever thought of as home.

Maddie watched the shock of her words reverberate through Boone's tall, rangy body, felt it in the tightening grip of his strong hand before he dropped hers, as if burned.

Boone turned his head away to study the house, his jaw tight, muscle jumping. The wind stirred his tawny hair. Rugged and muscular, he could have been formed from the harsh earth beneath him.

He belonged here, and she didn't. But she was here, and she would stay for the thirty days that Sam had required of her. Maddie Rose Collins wasn't a quitter, and she needed this place for a while. She turned her own gaze to follow his.

Crowning the low green hill dotted with pale limestone outcroppings, the house looked like everything a home should be. A place to cherish and shelter, nurture and enfold.

And it was hers, if she wanted it.

At this man's expense.

"Do you know why he did it?" she asked.

His laughter was a harsh bark. "I don't even know *what* he did yet." He shook his head. "Like a fool, I hoped he'd changed." Then he shot her a sideways glance. "Why did he leave the ranch to you?"

"He didn't leave me the ranch, just the house and one acre. He left the land to you and your brother."

Boone stared at her as if deciding whether to believe her. "I don't understand."

She tried to figure out how to explain what she didn't really understand herself. She knew a few facts now, but it was hard to accept the idea that the man who had fathered her had lied to her all her life. He was not Edward Collins, as she had known him, but a man named Dalton Wheeler, who had vanished from Morning Star thirty years before.

"He said it was a debt he owed my father."

"Who's your father?"

"He was known around here as Dalton Wheeler."

"Dalton Wheeler?" Blue eyes opened wide in shock. "He killed his stepfather."

*People think he killed his stepfather, but he didn't. He confessed and then vanished to save his mother from the consequences of what she'd done.* The words from Sam's letter echoed in Maddie's head.

"He didn't kill anyone. Your father's lawyer sent me proof."

Boone frowned. "He died before you would have been born, unless you're a lot older than you look."

"I'm twenty-eight. And he didn't die until four years ago. Only I knew him as Edward Collins."

"This was the old Wheeler place, all right, but Dad bought it fair and square after old Rose died."

"The letter said that Sam didn't know until years later that my father was alive."

Boone shook his head, his jaw working. "City girls don't belong here. Sam had no use for the last one who came."

"You say 'city girl' like it's some kind of curse word. What do you know about where I belong?"

He was right, though. She had driven halfway across the country and she still wasn't sure if she was crazy to be here. She had no life in Texas, no reason to stay.

But it was only temporary. She was beginning her life all over and she desperately needed time to think, to plan. Sam Gallagher had provided the place, and it had seemed as good as any to someone who'd spent her life on the move. In the meantime, her worst-case scenario was that she'd learn something about her father's past, have a month-long vacation, and a nest egg with which to start again.

But she hadn't counted on spending her vacation with a tall stranger who had shadows in his eyes. She looked back at him, seeing utter exhaustion in his unguarded gaze.

But not unguarded for long—not once he knew she was looking. "You can't stay here."

"I don't have any choice."

"You do. You can turn around and walk away. I'll pay you whatever you think you're owed."

She couldn't believe his nerve. Before she could think how to respond, another voice spoke up.

"None of this is her fault, Boone," said a tiny, redheaded old woman who Maddie hadn't seen approaching. "Now stop yelling and come inside, both of you. Sounds like Sam's put you both in a pretty pickle, and no amount of getting mad is going to get you out."

She turned to Maddie. "I'm Vondell Cartwright. I've been the housekeeper here since Moses was a pup. Don't mind Boone. He needs to go soak his head—'' she shot Boone a glare ''—and then sleep for a week.''

"Did you *know,* Vondell?" Boone's voice grated, his face harsh. "Why didn't you say something to me?"

"You just got here. You're exhausted. Besides, you know your daddy better than that. He never told anyone anything until he was ready. I knew he was spending a lot of time with his lawyer and that nice young private investigator Devlin Marlowe, but he didn't see fit to confide in me about his plans. Just asked me to hang around because you might need me."

She turned to Maddie. "I don't expect that you're used to this Texas heat. Come on inside, and let me get you a glass of iced tea. We can talk there, instead of standing in the noonday heat like mad dogs and Englishmen. You comin', Boone?" She turned away as if certain they'd follow.

Maddie shot a glance at Boone to see what he would do.

He stared at the house, then out over the pasture beyond it. Maddie thought then that there was something unutterably weary about him, something almost lost. She had no idea what to say to him, given the shocks they'd both received. Her temper drained away.

"I'm not planning to stay for good, but I can't leave yet. I have to stay for thirty days."

Boone studied her then, his gaze measuring. "Why?"

Maddie couldn't tell how she came out on his scale. "Your father asked me to stay here thirty days to decide if I want the place. If I don't, then only you can buy me out. If I let you do it sooner, the lawyer said the Caswells would get the house."

"Dalton's stepfather was a Caswell."

"And Buster Caswell used his fists on my grandmother until she feared for her life. I don't think you want them to get this place. I certainly don't."

"No one else is going to have this place, especially the Caswells. But you don't know what you're getting into. You'll be stir-crazy in a week."

"I'm a big girl. You let me worry about myself."

Boone looked away, his jaw pulsing. After a long silence, he nodded his head. "Fine, then. We'll just have to make do until it's over. I can stay out in the barn."

Maddie bristled. She'd been measured and found wanting, yet again. This time by a man who didn't even know her. "You don't have to stay in the barn. Surely that house is big enough for both of us for thirty days." Then her temper started to simmer again. "You don't know anything about me, but you've already decided my future."

His blue eyes didn't soften. "Can you honestly tell me you want to spend your life in a place like this?" A sweep of his arm took in the horizon and stark, sunbaked earth.

For as far as Maddie could see, there was not one

other house, certainly no theaters or fine restaurants or museums. And absolutely nowhere for her to use her skills as a chef. Of course she didn't want to stay. She would be gone as soon as the thirty days were over.

But Boone's pigheaded certainty galled her, and she would rise to the challenge. Like the optimist she'd always been, Maddie refused to make this less than an adventure, despite the glowering man beside her. She'd do better than endure this stay, and when she left to go back to her chosen environment, she'd have stories to tell for years.

Maddie the Cowgirl. It had a certain ring. She shook off her temper and, instead, smiled, lifting her gaze to Boone's startled look.

"No, I don't want to spend my life in a place like this. But don't write me off, Boone Gallagher. You may think you know city girls, but you've never met Maddie Rose Collins." She turned to follow Vondell, calling back over her shoulder in imitation. "You comin', Boone?"

When she glanced back, he was just standing there staring at her, hands on lean hips, shoulders broader than the Brooklyn Bridge. So rugged and handsome her mouth went dry.

"You're wrong, Maddie Rose. I know everything I need to know about you. You're a city girl, used to fine things and lots of entertainment. Bright lights and noise and bustle. You'll hate this place, just like—" He broke off.

"Just like who?"

"Never mind. Go on inside. I'll take care of the calf." He turned his back and headed away.

It was shaping up to be a long thirty days—stuck with Mr. Personality in the middle of nowhere, when all she had wanted was peace and quiet.

Ah, well. A good chef improvised with whatever ingredients she had at hand.

And Maddie Rose was a very good chef.

It felt good to Boone to have the land under his feet again. He'd known when he shipped off on the tanker that it was only temporary, but after his wife Helen had died, it was as far as he could get from this place where so much had gone wrong. An oil tanker was a big switch for a former Navy SEAL, but he hadn't cared. He'd have gone to the moon if he could have found a ride.

The calluses on his hands served him well, since he hadn't come home carrying gloves in his back pocket—something that had once been second nature. He'd found a rope and supplies in the closest barn and tied up the cow so she couldn't interfere while he freed the calf. Now he carefully doctored the cuts with antibiotic salve.

"There, little guy," he said, letting the calf up.

The calf scrambled away about ten feet, eyeing Boone with suspicion before seeking the shelter of his mother's side. Boone approached her carefully and slipped the rope off her neck, then slapped her on the rump and shooed them both away.

Barbwire left lying on the ground inside a pasture? His father would have fired a man on the spot for that. Just how bad were things? And where were all the ranch hands?

Boone rubbed his eyes, wishing he had his old straw hat. He'd walked away from everything when he left, and Sam had probably burned it all. But he was too tired to look for any of his belongings now. He needed to hit the sack and sleep around the clock.

*Why did it all go so wrong, Dad? Did you hate us so much that you couldn't even leave us the only place that ever felt like home?*

Instead, Sam had left it to a woman who couldn't possibly appreciate it. A woman who didn't belong. But Maddie had said it was payment for a wrong Sam had done her father. What had Sam done?

Too many questions. Too much hot sun. Too little sleep. The house wavered in his vision.

*Get inside, Boone. You can move to the barn tomorrow. Right now you're no good to anyone without some sleep.*

But first he had to see if he could find Sam's foreman, Jim Caskey, or any of the hands. He needed to understand where things stood. Placing one foot in front of the other, Boone didn't look back toward the house that had once been all he'd wanted of heaven…until the day it had turned into hell.

## Chapter Two

When Maddie stepped inside the back door and saw the kitchen, it only confirmed her first impression. This house would never make the pages of *Architectural Digest,* but she could swear that she felt the pulse of generations in this room.

To think that her grandmother had cooked here—even saying the word *grandmother* gave Maddie a charge. To a woman who had never known any family except her mother and father, lost in a plane crash four years ago, the concept was almost unimaginable.

*Why, Daddy? Why did you lie to me?* She'd had days to ponder, but the betrayal still seemed enormous. She hurt. She didn't know how to forgive him.

Maddie ran a hand across the counter and wondered if her grandmother's hand had touched this very spot. For a moment she went still, as though by listening carefully, she might hear the whispers of her father's hidden past.

Suddenly, Maddie realized that Vondell was watching her closely. She jerked her hand away. "I'm sorry."

"No need to be, child. You look like you've seen a ghost."

Maddie felt like she had. "Did you know my grandmother Wheeler?"

"Old Rose?" Vondell nodded. "Not well, but everyone knew the story. After Dalton—" She fell silent. "Well, never mind about that."

Maddie's heart stuttered. These people believed her father to be a murderer. "I know what you're thinking, but he didn't kill anyone. Sam's lawyer was satisfied about that."

"Well, it's not my place to be talking about Dalton Wheeler." Vondell turned away toward the refrigerator, dropping ice cubes into a glass. "I'll get you that tea that I promised you."

"You don't believe me."

"Hon, I— It's just that for years, everyone knew— Well, it'll take some getting used to, is all. But it's old news. It really doesn't matter."

"It does matter. It matters to me. The man I knew never even got a traffic ticket. Did you know him?"

The tiny redhead shook her head.

"That was before I moved here. It was a long time ago, Maddie. Water under the bridge."

Vondell was being kind, but Maddie suddenly felt very much alone, very much the stranger here. And sorry she had agreed to come. But she wasn't the only one struggling to adjust. She remembered the brief, unguarded glance she'd had into Boone's blue eyes. That man had been hurt badly by his father. Now she was helping to hurt him more. *Why did you do this to me, Sam Gallagher?* How could a man who would seek to make peace with a total stranger use that stranger to hurt his own son?

"Here, child, sit down and drink this tea." Vondell placed the glass in her hand.

Maddie took a sip, vaguely registering the cool freshness of mint. She watched moisture bead on the outside and thought of her daydream of porch swings and iced tea. This sure wasn't the vacation she'd expected. Her head jerked up.

"Why didn't he just give the house to his sons, no matter what he owed my father?"

"Sam was powerfully troubled in his last weeks, and he seemed determined to make things right."

"But why didn't Boone know about this already?"

"Sam waited too long to let anyone look for him." Vondell's eyes darkened. "Sam has a lot to answer for, the way he treated those boys. I can't explain Sam Gallagher to you, Maddie. I doubt anyone could. He was a complicated man who was never the same after his wife, Jenny, died. He destroyed a whole family in his selfish grief, just flat abandoned Boone, who was only fourteen at the time, and tried to have Mitch arrested when any fool could see it was an accident.

"Sure, Mitch was driving crazy after Sam threw him out because he was drinking, but the accident was just lousy luck. The roads were slick when Jenny took off after Mitch, and a truck dodging Mitch's skid hit her. I just keep thinking about that boy out on a dark highway, his mama dying in his arms. Mitch loved Jenny as much as Boone, as much as Sam. He needed his family then. But Sam wouldn't even let him attend his own mother's funeral." Sorrow fell heavily across her worn features. "We never saw Mitch again."

Vondell stared at the scarred table, shaking her head. "I've never seen anyone lose his mind in grief like that. If it hadn't been for Boone, Sam would have lost this place, too. Young as he was, Boone kept this place running until Sam took the reins again. But Sam was never the same after that, and he lost two fine sons anyone would be proud to claim."

Vondell brushed away angry tears, her eyes sparking. "I kept trying to talk sense into him, but a more stubborn man never walked the face of this planet. When Boone left, I think Sam realized some of what he'd lost, but he just hardened his heart and went on like those boys had never existed. If I hadn't called Boone back when Sam had his heart attack a few years ago, I don't guess they would ever have spoken again. And the way things turned out, maybe Boone would have been better off.''

''What do you mean?''

Vondell rose and reached for her apron, tying it around her waist. ''That's not really for me to tell. If Boone wants to tell you, that's his business.''

Maddie shook her head. ''I doubt Boone will want to tell me the time of day, and I don't think I blame him. The best thing I can do is to pass my thirty days and get out of his way.''

Vondell turned to face her. ''You don't think you'll want this place?''

Maddie had to smile at that. ''No offense, but I can't imagine it. There's not much demand for a chef in Morning Star, I don't think.''

The older woman's eyebrows rose. ''You mean you're one of those fancy cooks like Julia Child or something? You cook with leeks and kiwi fruit and that sort of thing?''

''I cook with all sorts of ingredients. I'm not a snob about food. I just want it fresh and wholesome.''

''Well, that about sums up my cooking. Most of what I cook comes from my garden and the stock raised here.''

''You have a garden?'' Maddie's pulse sped up. Her dream was her own restaurant, with a greenhouse where she could control the quality of her food more closely. ''What do you grow?''

''The usual stuff. Onions, tomatoes, cucumbers, beans and such.''

"Do you grow your own herbs?"

Vondell smiled. "Hon, these men around here only care about meat and potatoes. Salt and pepper's plenty for them. I got to work hard to make them eat a salad."

Maddie's vision of fresh arugula, of pots of oregano and rosemary and chives, vanished as quickly as it had come. "I'd love to see your garden. I've wished for my own, but space is at a premium in the city, even if you could get good sun with all the buildings."

Vondell cocked her head, oddly hesitant. "You wouldn't happen to know how to make those little radish roses, would you?"

Maddie smiled. "I can make carrot garnishes to die for, too."

Vondell cackled. "I'd like to see Boone's face if I put a radish rose on his plate. You gotta teach me."

"I'm not so sure I need to antagonize Boone right now."

"Aw, hon, once Boone gets some sleep and has a chance to think about it, he'll be all right. Besides, this place could use a little shaking up." She grinned like a conspirator, practically rubbing her hands with glee.

Maddie couldn't help returning her smile. It was going to be a long thirty days. No sense making it grim, as well. Robert used to tell her that she wasn't serious enough, that her sense of play was like a child's.

Well, she was here for a vacation, here to remember who Maddie was. She'd stay out of Boone's way as much as possible, but she was through making herself into something she wasn't.

She'd sworn, after Robert, never to get involved with a man who couldn't accept her as she was. Not that getting involved with Boone Gallagher was even remotely possible or desirable, no matter how handsome he might be.

Boone walked into the horse barn, a scrap of barbwire in hand, looking for Sam's foreman. "Jim?"

No answer, except the whinny from a stall down the way. Boone stuck the length of wire into a trash barrel and headed in the direction of the sound, wondering if it could really be Gulliver, Sam's horse.

It was.

"Hey, buddy," he soothed, holding out his hand for the big gelding to sniff. Gulliver's head lifted, then he passed his muzzle over Boone's hand, the soft whuffle of his breath warm on Boone's palm.

While he stroked the old roan, Boone's mind wandered to all the times he'd seen his father on the back of this horse. Sam had loved this horse with a fierceness with which he loved no one else once Jenny died. If Boone could have claimed half that love for himself, they could have built on that. But when Mom died, his father had crawled inside his grief and slammed the door shut. There had been no room for anyone else.

*Gallagher men love only once,* Sam always said, and Boone had vowed to be different. If the price of such a love was to cast away everything else if you lost it, abandon everyone who needed you most, the price was too high.

Boone had succeeded too well at his vow. He had married a woman who had pursued him like a trophy—a senator's daughter who saw a chest full of medals and a sparkling future. The wounded warrior, weary of roaming the globe, had no home to which he could return. He had seized the opportunity to make a new start and had counted himself lucky.

They had both been wrong.

He had come to care for Helen, but he hadn't loved her the way she'd needed. And then he'd yanked her out of her world and brought her to Texas after Sam's first heart attack. Helen's heart had dried to nothing in the harsh Texas wind.

And she'd died fleeing the life that was killing her, day by lonely day.

He'd tried to help. Tried to be enough, torn between two people who couldn't stand each other— an old man who'd written him off years ago and a wife who was pining for a life that was light-years away. He'd given her money that he couldn't spare so she could go home and visit, too proud to let her daddy foot the bill. It had been a futile effort to help her recharge her batteries so she could endure coming back to a place that she hated. Every visit back east only made things worse, though, because Boone knew by then that this was the only place *he* would ever be home.

The last time he'd seen her, she'd been carrying

his baby—and had never even told him. His hope for a family died two years ago with his wife in a sailing accident.

With her old college flame at the helm.

Gulliver stirred and stamped, and Boone realized his hand was knotted in the gelding's mane. Easing his fingers apart, Boone stepped away. The past was the past. He would spend his future alone because he had never figured out how to manage love.

But he had the ranch, and that would be enough.

Gulliver nuzzled at his hand. ''Anybody exercising you, boy?'' Suddenly Boone realized that he needed the ride, too. Needed to feel the wind and the sun, a good horse beneath him. He headed for the tack room to get Gulliver's bridle.

He stopped in his tracks in front of the tree that held Sam's saddle. His hand hovered over the leather, and happier days rushed back. Memories of being lifted into the saddle in front of his father, too young to ride his pony where they were headed. His mother would wave to them as they turned toward the pastures, where Sam would pass along to his son the legacy of a lifetime's hard work. Mitch had never felt the ranch sing in his blood, but Boone had soaked up every scrap of knowledge Sam wanted to share. He had been an eager student, and he had thought he'd never leave this place.

Boone looked around the tack room and wished for his own saddle, uneasy at using Sam's. Jim's was missing from its tree; there were two others, neither big enough for Boone.

His gaze returned to his father's saddle, a symbol of all that Sam had once been, all that Boone had once hoped. In that moment, memories, bad and good, jostled for room in his chest. But what pierced through them all was a sharp ache for what could now never be.

Sam was gone, without a word to the son who had once thought the sun rose and set in him. They would never heal the pain that was now the legacy of this place.

But one thing Boone knew, deep in his bones. He loved this place, needed this land. If it hadn't become his in the way he'd dreamed as a kid—worked with his father and then handed down with love—it was still his. Not the house yet, but even that would come in time. And his brother would be found, no matter how long Boone had to look.

He would reclaim this place for what was left of Jenny Gallagher's dreams. He had spent enough years wandering; he had been rootless too long. He would have no one to pass it on to, but perhaps Mitch would.

Boone was home now, where he belonged. And here he would stay.

He picked up Sam's saddle, and with it, his own lost dreams. He had plenty to do to restore the neglect he could see all around him. Whatever the price was to buy Maddie out, he would find a way to meet it.

He would ignore the gypsy with sass in her eyes and too little sense. He would give her a wide berth, be gone before she rose and back after she slept. And if his hands itched a little to touch remembered curves, well, he'd often been off on missions or at sea for months at a time. Boone knew how to control himself, and he would, for an instinct that had kept him alive in some hairy situations whispered that this woman could be trouble with a capital *T*. She was beautiful and totally out of place. She was what stood between him and the home he'd never wanted to leave.

Whatever her claim, whatever wrong Sam was trying to right, he would simply wait her out. She would stay her thirty days, he'd definitely see to that—the Caswells would get this place over his dead body. But everything he loved about the ranch was everything she'd hate.

It was no place for city girls. Maddie would be gone soon enough.

Maddie stretched and yawned, surprised that she'd fallen asleep. She'd only meant to lie down for a minute, but the bright sun had gone far past the window of this lovely room.

Vondell had told her that it was once Jenny's sewing room and, like much of the house, Sam had left it almost a shrine. Vondell had wanted to put Maddie in the master bedroom, but Maddie couldn't imagine a move more calculated to raise Boone's hackles than to take over Sam's quarters or the room that Vondell said had belonged to Boone's brother Mitch. She was only temporary, and this was the only room left. The downside was that Boone's room was at this end of the hallway and there was only one bathroom—but neither could be helped.

She liked this room, its old wallpaper dotted with tiny yellow roses. White Priscilla curtains over the windows matched a white chenille bedspread on the twin bed where she lay. The chenille had made her smile at first sight. It was just one of the things about Maddie that had driven Robert crazy, that she loved vintage clothes and wore them whenever she could. Stored in her apartment in New York was one whole closet of odds and ends she'd picked up, from broad-shouldered suits and tiny hats with veils to a genuine flapper dress and a big brown mouton coat.

Among her prize possessions was a lilac chenille robe that she'd brought along with her. It wasn't sexy and it sure wasn't glamorous, but Maddie loved the peacock design spreading across the back, the chenille feathers topping the patch pockets in front. She didn't wear it often because it wouldn't stand up to daily wear, but whenever Maddie was troubled, bundling into that robe made her feel protected and coddled.

It was the kind of robe she could imagine a grandmother wearing…a grandmother who would have fixed her a cup of hot chocolate when she spent the night, who would have bustled around the kitchen in the morning.

Maddie had never had a grandmother, never known any relatives other than her parents. Her mother had been an orphan, and her father's past had been a dark hole at the core of their lives, a subject never to be discussed. It was simply the way things were, and the child-Maddie had never questioned it. The woman-Maddie now knew why.

Her father had moved them from place to place all of her life, constantly reminding her of the folly of depending upon anyone but herself. Maddie had had little choice. At the succession of schools where she'd always been the new kid, she'd been too eccentric, too colorful, too smart. She had never fit in, but she hadn't let it matter.

Until Robert. After losing her only family, she'd been alone and scared and had wanted desperately to do things right so she wouldn't be alone anymore. But she'd lost too much of herself in the process.

Now Maddie was alone again. Though a part of her was shocked and furious with the father she'd always loved deeply, she recognized that he had been right. She was a fool to depend upon anyone but herself.

And if she ever got involved with a man again— which wouldn't be soon—she swore it would only be with someone who didn't want to change her, someone who liked Maddie for exactly who she was.

Her stomach rumbled. The aroma wafting up the stairwell reminded her that it had been early this morning since she'd last had food. But downstairs, she would have to contend with Boone and this mess that Sam had left her.

Maddie straightened and shook her hair in defiance. The glowering giant would be her test at standing up for herself. She ran a quick brush through her hair and bounded down the stairs.

Boone toed his boots off outside the back door, leaving them on the porch out of years of long habit. His mother had trained them well.

Something smelled terrific, and he was starving. He and Gulliver had enjoyed their run, and he had found Jim and worked out tomorrow's plans. There were problems here, for sure, but nothing that couldn't be handled by buckling down to hard work, something he'd never minded. Both Jim and Sonny Chavez, a hand who worked as needed, had seemed glad to see someone at the helm again. Now all Boone wanted was a shower, something to eat and a bed to fall into until sunup.

When he opened the back door, laughter greeted him, Vondell's rusty cackle mingling with a full, rich laugh that rippled across his hearing and landed a sucker punch to his gut. Maddie laughed the way she talked: throaty and low. It was a laugh filled with life and sparkle. Their backs were turned to him, both bent over the counter, studying something intently.

"I swear, I will never get the hang of this, gal."

"Sure you will, Vondell. You've already got the top petals right. You're a quick study."

He could see one side of Vondell's face and the quick blush that stained her cheeks.

Blush? *Vondell?*

He closed the door behind him, and both jumped

and whirled. He couldn't tell who looked more guilty.

"Boone, I didn't expect—uh, supper's not quite ready."

Boone glanced back and forth, wondering what it was that Vondell hid behind her back. "Didn't mean to startle you," he replied. Despite feeling as if his bones could sink into the floor, curiosity tickled at his resolve to head straight for the shower. "You all right?"

"Oh—sure—sure. Never better," Vondell blustered.

Maddie simply watched him, chin up but eyes sparkling.

"Need some help?"

"Me?" Vondell squeaked. "Why, no, not at all. Uh, Maddie's helping me."

Boone turned to study Maddie. "You know how to cook, do you?"

She fought a grin that he didn't understand. "A little."

Vondell shot her a shocked glance. "But, Maddie, you're a—"

"A quick learner," Maddie supplied.

"Now I don't know why you're being so modest. Maddie here is a genuine gourmet chef from New York."

Boone watched a shadow cross over the mischief in Maddie's eyes. "Is that right? Well, not much call for gourmet chefs in this part of Texas. There is The

Dinner Bell over on the highway, but I'm afraid it won't quite measure up to your standards.''

Maddie's chin jutted upward. ''Good food is good food, wherever it's served.''

''So why would a gourmet chef leave a fancy restaurant in New York to come to this little burg? Who's doing the cooking while you're rescuing calves?''

Maddie's eyes darkened for a moment, but then came the sparks. Had he been standing closer, his hide would have been singed. Boone decided he liked the sparks better than the shadows.

''I had a small share in a restaurant, but my partner bought me out. I'm trying to decide whether to accept one of several offers or open my own place when I go back.''

''And they'll wait for you to decide? You must be good.''

Maddie locked her gaze on his and gave him a slow, wicked smile that could suck the breath out of a man's lungs. ''I'm very good.''

Boone couldn't respond yet. He was still trying to draw a good breath. ''Well—'' He stirred, slapping his hands on denim-covered thighs. ''Guess I'd better grab a shower before Vondell throws my supper out.''

As he crossed the room, Vondell turned her body in tandem with his motion so her back stayed hidden. Boone shot her a curious glance, but Vondell only blushed again.

Vondell, the drill sergeant, blushing. Would wonders never cease? Boone mounted the stairs with tired steps, still wondering what the two of them were hiding.

But not sure he really wanted to know.

Maddie thought she'd choke to death on her iced tea at the look on Boone's face when he saw the radish roses decorating his plate. She wanted to laugh so badly that her side ached, but she was afraid it would hurt Vondell's feelings. Vondell fidgeted in her chair, waiting for his reaction. She'd tried to throw them in the compost crock, but Maddie had stood guard over them before she could succeed.

"Well, don't just sit there like a bump on a log." Vondell went on the offensive. "Eat your supper before it gets cold."

Boone cleared his throat. "What are these?"

Vondell colored. "You're thirty years old and you can't recognize a radish? I thought you injured your back in the service, not your brain. They're radish roses. You can eat 'em or not."

He shot a look at Maddie. Maddie gave him no help. He cleared his throat again. "They're, uh, real pretty, Vondell. Kinda decorates the plate."

"Aw, go ahead and laugh. You know you want to."

He frowned. "I do not. I just don't know quite what to do with them."

"You eat 'em, you big galoot. Just like you eat any old radish."

Boone took a cautious bite. His eyebrows lifted. "Don't taste any different."

Vondell harrumphed. "Damn fool idea. Don't know why you didn't let me throw them out, Maddie."

"You said you wanted to learn how to do them, and you did a superb job." She shot him a glare that would have melted lead. "Didn't she, Boone?"

"Uh, yeah—yeah, you did, Vondell. They're, uh, real pretty." Affection for the older woman shone from his eyes. "And they taste just fine."

"Aw, get on with you. Just eat your chicken-fried steak," she grumbled, but her cheeks were flushed again. She rose from the table and headed toward the sink. "After all these years of cooking for men, don't know why I ever wanted to try such a thing."

Boone glowered at Maddie like this was all her fault. Maddie simply shrugged her shoulders and popped another radish in her mouth.

"This meal is wonderful, Vondell," she said.

"Too plain for what you're used to, I'm sure."

Boone spoke up. "You don't ever have to apologize for your cooking. I used to dream about it."

Vondell turned, eyes shining. Maddie took a new look at Boone.

"Is that right?"

He nodded, finishing another huge bite. "Sometimes I thought if I could just have one more slice of your chocolate cake or one of your biscuits, I could die a happy man."

"Flatterer," Vondell protested, but her pleasure

shone from her face. "You're just wondering if I made your favorite chocolate cake."

Boone smiled and suddenly looked about fifteen years old. Hope flared in his blue eyes, and Maddie wondered where this Boone had been hiding. "Did you?"

"Of course I did. Think you can stay awake long enough to eat some?"

Then Maddie finally looked—really looked—at Boone, seeing that though his golden hair still glistened with moisture from the shower and his angular face was clean-shaven, exhaustion lined his face and settled heavily on his frame.

"It's close to two days now since you left to come here, right? A body can't live on catnaps taken on airplanes." Vondell clucked her tongue.

"I'll make it fine." His tone said he didn't need mothering. "I used to have to stay awake longer than this on some missions." But then the smile flashed once again. "But I do believe I'd sleep a lot better after a slice of your chocolate cake."

Glowing with pleasure, Vondell turned away to get him a piece.

And Maddie tried not to wonder how it would feel to have him smile that way at her.

## Chapter Three

What was that?

Maddie stirred, disoriented, wondering why there were cattle in her apartment. Tempted to roll over and go back to sleep, she suddenly remembered.

She wasn't in New York. She was in Morning Star, Texas.

Maddie sat up and shook her head.

Stretching, she yawned, then rolled out of bed. Motion outside the window caught her eye, and she moved toward it.

Through the open window, she smelled the sweetest scent imaginable and looked around to see what it might be. Honeysuckle in abundance covered the white picket fence that delineated a yard around the house. Just past it, she saw the source of the noises she'd heard. Cattle being loaded into a trailer by two men intent on their work. The man with his back to her was a stranger.

Facing her was the man she'd fallen asleep thinking about last night.

Boone. But a different Boone. A relaxed Boone, at ease with who he was and what he was doing—not a trace of the growling stranger. Maddie couldn't help staring. He might not be Prince Charming, but he was one very attractive man. She'd felt the power of those muscles that she saw moving beneath the worn fabric of his chambray shirt. Broad shoulders…lean hips…long legs filling jeans so old the seams were white.

The man she saw could make a woman forget that cowboys weren't her style.

Maddie shivered. Then she lectured herself, trying to forget the feel of his strength when he'd come to her rescue, the unaccustomed sense of safety she'd had in his arms.

*The man can't stand you, Maddie.* He'd made it clear that he would count the days until she was gone.

She didn't know how they'd tiptoe around each other for thirty days. But if she saw no more than she'd seen of him so far, it might work just fine. He had headed upstairs last night, the minute he'd finished eating. Given the state of his exhaustion, she had no idea how he was even standing now, much less already up and working.

Anyway, she was here to think, to figure out

whether to accept the job offers she had or to try to come up with the money for her own place. She had places to go, people to meet. She didn't need the distraction.

But that didn't mean that she couldn't admire the view. When Boone smiled at something the other man said, she went still, leaning on the windowsill and letting her eyes fill with the sight of a man who would make any woman's heart skip a beat or two.

Lost in dreamland, she didn't react fast enough when those blue eyes looked up and locked on hers. Boone's face tightened into a frown, and she regretted the loss of that easy grin. But he didn't stop looking, and for a moment that spun out forever, Maddie couldn't seem to move.

Then she realized that her short silk nightgown left little to the imagination. She took a quick step backward and grabbed for her robe the second she was out of sight.

Coffee. She needed to get her brain clicking before she thought again about the power of Boone Gallagher's smile.

"Aaayyiii, Boone. *She's* the one Sam left the house to?" Sonny Chavez clucked his tongue. *"Muy bonita."*

"You're married. And she won't be here long. She's going to sell the house to me as soon as she's satisfied Sam's requirement."

"Got under your skin, eh?"

"She's a looker, all right. But not my type."

"I haven't seen you look at a woman like that since—"

Boone's jaw tightened. "I'm not looking now."

"You'll play hell finding one like that around here. Where'd she come from?"

"The city." Boone spat out the words.

"Which city?"

"It doesn't matter. City women don't stick it out here. She'll be gone soon."

"But while she's here…"

Boone shot him a glare. "Can it, Sonny. I'm not looking for a woman." It had been a very long time, but no way. And not this woman.

"Hell, Boone. When you gonna get over a woman who—"

"Watch it, Sonny."

"I'm sorry. But Helen was gone the moment she got here. You did everything you could. You turned yourself inside out, trying to please both her and your dad. It wasn't your fault."

"I don't want to talk about it." He slid the lock closed on the trailer and pulled off his gloves. "I'm going to get a cup of coffee before I leave. See you this afternoon."

Sonny just shook his head. "Helen was never going to be satisfied. It ever occur to you that maybe she wasn't good enough for you? Maybe it wasn't you who screwed up?"

"No. It didn't. Period." Boone turned and walked toward the house. Helen had been effervescent when they'd married and for many months after, until—

Until he'd turned her life upside down and taken her to live in a nowhere town with an old man who disliked her on sight.

And she'd never been the same again. She'd be alive today if he hadn't dragged her halfway across the country out of a sense of duty to a man who didn't care enough even to let his sons know when he was dying.

*Aw, bag it, Boone. It's an old subject.* He had put it to rest until *she* showed up.

She. The looker. Wearing that tiny scrap of lace struggling to cover curves that Boone could still feel against his body.

Damn. Radish roses and scraps of lace. It was shaping up to be the longest thirty days of his life.

Boone pulled off his boots outside the kitchen door and stepped inside in his socks, heading for the coffeepot that Vondell kept going all day—

And was blindsided by the curves he'd just been trying to banish from his brain.

Maddie stumbled, and he reached out to steady her, the thin silk kimono transmitting her body heat straight into his palms.

He jerked away. "Whoa—where's the fire?"

Maddie's gray eyes were velvet-soft and sleepy. All too easily, he could imagine that look under other circumstances. He quickly shifted his gaze away and downward.

Big mistake. The midnight-blue kimono gapped at the cleavage, and he could see lace clinging to the shape he'd admired a few minutes before.

Only now, he wasn't yards away. He was within inches. His fingers flexed, itching to touch, to see if what he remembered—

He cleared a throat gone suddenly dry. "Uh…I came to get coffee."

"That's where I was headed. I'll pour you a cup," she murmured in that low, throaty tone that detoured right past his brain into far more dangerous regions. She turned away and crossed the small space, standing on tiptoes to reach two mugs.

And there they were. Those long, long legs that had walked through his dreams more than once last night. The kimono clung to hips that definitely belonged to a woman, the fabric barely brushing the tops of her thighs—

"…or sugar?" Red highlights shone from her dark hair when her head swung around.

*Get a grip, Boone.* Jaw tightening, he bit off the words. "Black. Just black. You don't need to wait on me."

Mug in hand, she crossed the floor, her full lips curving. "Oh, please. Don't thank me so sweetly." She was waking up now, her eyes shining with challenge. She handed him the mug.

"Thanks." Boone sipped too quickly, scalding his tongue.

Maddie's lips curved higher, drawing his attention like moth to a flame.

"Got—got work to do." Before his wings incinerated, Boone headed for the door.

The hounds of hell nipped at his heels, disguised in the form of a sassy, sexy woman.

Twenty-nine days and counting.

Maddie leaned against the fence, watching the baby nuzzle its mother's belly, rooting around to nurse. The mare kicked out one leg and shifted. Finally, the baby latched onto a nipple, and the mare settled in.

Maddie smiled and laid her head against the railing, sighing out loud. How sweet.

The Border collie pup that had followed her made a sound, and Maddie looked down to see him happily chewing her shoelace.

"You little devil. What am I going to do with you? Isn't your mother calling?" She reached down and lifted him up, nuzzling his head with her jaw while she scratched beneath his chin. He whimpered with pleasure. "Beggar."

He caught a lock of her hair and began chewing on it. Maddie laughed, and he scrambled closer, his little claws tickling her neck. Maddie sat down, giggling, then rolled back on the grass and held him against her chest.

Boone watched her from the barn, wondering who this woman really was. This morning's siren had turned into something else altogether. Seeing her so unguarded, so much like a fresh-faced girl, did things to his insides—things he didn't want to think about.

But he couldn't help smiling as the pup scrambled

across her chest and began rooting at her neck. Maddie rolled on the ground, giggling like a ten-year-old. Then she scooped up the pup and hugged him hard.

Lucky pup.

Boone knew that it was foolish, even while he was walking toward her, but he just had to figure this woman out. Then he could write her off and forget her.

Maddie felt the shadow cross her body before she looked up, but somehow she'd already known it was Boone. Something about him seemed to tickle her antennae every time he was anywhere nearby.

She craned her head up. He looked ten feet tall. But he wasn't frowning, so that was a nice change.

"Hi."

"Hi," he answered. "Devil bothering you?"

"Is that his name?"

Boone shrugged, then knelt at her side. The pup abandoned her in a heartbeat, rooting at Boone's hand. "Seems to fit his sense of mischief."

She had to agree. "It really does." She couldn't take her eyes away from those strong fingers, the wide palms. Envying the puppy who received the stroking. Remembering how those hands had felt in her all-too-brief encounter with Boone Gallagher's potent physical charms.

*Maybe we could just have a little fling while I'm here.*

Maddie shook her head roughly. *Good grief, Mad-*

*die. You're insane.* Besides, she wasn't the "fling" type.

"Why are you here, Maddie?"

She sighed. Back to that. "You know why."

"How can you just leave your life and come down here for a month?"

Maddie wasn't ready to discuss her failures with Robert, so she turned the tables. "How could you leave for so long?"

He stiffened. He probably didn't like being on the receiving end, she thought. But she noticed that his hands stayed gentle on the puppy falling asleep against that broad chest.

Then he met her gaze, shadows in his eyes. "Long story. Nothing you'd want to hear."

"Maybe I would."

"And maybe I don't want to talk about it." His tone made it clear that she was trespassing.

But something in Maddie wanted to dig past his secrets. Find out who this man was. "Where were you?"

Boone huffed out a breath. "Don't give up easy, do you?" He shook his head, then stared out in the distance. "Serving my country."

"Doing what?"

"Things I don't want to discuss."

"I'm sorry."

He stared at her. "Why?"

"Because..." She gestured around her. "You had to leave this." Her gaze returned to his. "And because I think it hurt your heart."

Boone wasn't sure what unsettled him most. That she saw too clearly his weary soul, or that she thought the ranch was a place to cherish. But he did know he didn't like how she saw too much.

"Wouldn't think this place would look like much to a woman like you."

"It has its own beauty. A little light on the amenities, if you need bright lights and noise."

"And you do, don't you?" He watched her closely.

"Why do you think you know anything about me, Boone? And who are you to tell me what I like and don't like?" Her chin jutted out and those gray eyes flashed.

Damn, he wanted to kiss away that stubborn line of her lips. But he was already sure that it wouldn't be enough to cure this growing fascination.

"Let's just say that I know only certain women can handle a place like this, and you aren't one of them. You don't belong here, Maddie Collins. You'd never stick."

She crossed her arms over her chest. "Good thing I've sworn off men like you for good. I don't have to care what you think."

"What do you mean, 'men like me'?"

"Doesn't feel too good, does it?" She cocked her head and studied him.

Boone couldn't decide whether to laugh or argue. Sass and a sharp mind—a dangerous combination. And altogether too intriguing.

"Boone, come here—quick!" Sonny called out.

"We've got a break in the fence line and cows out on the road."

He handed the puppy back to Maddie and rose quickly. "Anybody ever say you got a mouth on you, Maddie Rose?"

Her gray eyes crackled with energy. "Not yet—" Her smile went wide and way too inviting. "But thank you."

Boone shook his head, but when he walked away, he was grinning.

Maddie crossed the front porch after her evening walk. Dinner—or supper, as they called it around here—had been strained, the silences outweighing the conversation. Vondell asked questions about Boone's assessment of the ranch and about Maddie's life, her gambit to have each of them speak to the other failing miserably. Boone had reverted to the Man of Few Words, listening when Maddie spoke, responding to Vondell, but initiating no conversation himself.

Maddie herself had mostly sat uncharacteristically quiet, all too aware of the man sitting across the table. An enigma, he was, and one Maddie shouldn't want to solve. Her curiosity had gotten her in hot water all too often in her life. Boone stirred it up again. Though he hid it well, a deep sadness peered from those blue eyes. Yet true affection shone from his gaze when he looked at Vondell. With the ranch hands, he seemed relaxed. Only when she was around did he turn into a block of stone. This afternoon, it had almost seemed as if he was teasing her, but tonight the glowering stranger had returned.

*Can you blame him, Maddie? You waltzed into this place and stole his home.*

No. She hadn't stolen it. Sam Gallagher had given it away. Very soon Boone would have it back. As soon as she could possibly make it happen. This "vacation" had derailed on its very first day.

Yet the peace and quiet she had longed for was certainly abundant. Well, maybe not the peace—but definitely the quiet. It was almost eerie. Night sounds she didn't recognize had kept her awake longer than she would have liked.

Maddie stepped onto the porch and turned around, struck anew by the vista: gentle hills rolling on to the sunset; the only sounds, the wind, the soft lowing of cattle, the excited barking of a dog. She drew in a deep breath, realizing how her heartbeat slowed in time with the rhythm of a place that still bore the look of its past. If she ignored the power lines, she could be looking at this country as it was a hundred years ago.

Too slow for her, that was for sure. She had a lot of life to live yet—if only she could figure out how she wanted to do it. But still…there was something about this place that made her curious. She couldn't help trying to picture her father here, as a boy and young man. Couldn't help wondering about her grandmother…and those who had come before Rose. Sam's letter had said that generations of Wheelers had fought weather and Indians and hard times to keep this place. Closing her eyes, Maddie searched inside herself for a sense of connection, but nothing answered.

Maybe someone in Morning Star could tell her about her family. She'd ask Vondell.

Maddie opened the screen door and headed toward the kitchen. Just before she got there, she heard Boone's voice.

"What's the name of that investigator, Vondell? The one looking for Mitch?"

"Devlin Marlowe. He's out of Houston. Nice young fella, smart as a whip."

"You got his number?"

"No, but I'm sure it's on Sam's desk somewhere. Want me to look?"

"I'll look. I need to go over the books, anyway." He paused. "Guess I'd better go ask City Girl if it's all right, since it's *her* house, not mine."

"It's not her fault, Boone."

"I know it's not. I just—" A muffled curse was followed by a sigh. "I just wish I understood why he did it."

He sounded more weary than angry. Maddie settled back on her heels and wondered if she should turn around, or if she could make it to the stairs without being heard. Beneath her, a floorboard squeaked.

Boone stepped out into the hallway. "Want to join us, Big Ears?"

"I'm sorry. I didn't mean to eavesdrop. I was headed to my room."

"Well, while you're here, why don't you enlighten us?"

"I don't know much." She stepped around the door.

"Tell us what you do know. What is this debt Sam owed your father?"

"I don't really think—"

"You come in here and take my home, and I don't even deserve an explanation?"

Maddie's temper simmered. She tried to think up a simple answer. "He said it was because he should have looked for my father when he first knew he was alive."

"When did he find out?"

"I don't know. All I know is that it was before your mother died."

"Why didn't he look for Dalton?"

Maddie hesitated. "I'm not sure you'll want to hear it."

Boone's expression was wry. "I was just a kid then. How could it mean anything to me? Or am I wrong? Is it something he said about me? Maybe he just wanted me not to have this place so bad that he was grasping at straws."

"It's not about you. Listen—maybe it's not a good idea right now."

"So you're the one who decides what I need to know and when?"

"Boone—" Vondell cautioned.

He held up a hand. "No. I want to know." His gaze narrowed, tension invading his frame. "She comes down here to play lady of the manor for a month, inserting herself where she's not wanted, and then she eavesdrops on a private conversation. She has answers I need in order to understand maybe just a little of why my father hated me enough to do this—and she refuses to answer because *she,* who doesn't know a damn thing about any of us, doesn't think I'm ready to hear it!''

He crossed the kitchen floor and came to stand beside her. Maddie held her ground.

''Let me tell you something, City Girl. I've known since I was fourteen years old that my father didn't give a damn about me, that the only person who ever meant anything to him was my mother. He beat the hell out of my brother, then tried to have him arrested for murder, then crawled up inside his grief and didn't care what happened to anyone on this ranch.

''My mother was a good woman. The very best. She lived her life to love people. Her legacy was that love, and Sam perverted everything she stood for. But I survived. It made me a stronger person.''

He leaned closer, and Maddie met his gaze without flinching, seeing within those blue eyes pain of a magnitude she'd never in her life experienced.

''There's nothing you can tell me that's going to hurt me. I quit letting Sam Gallagher hurt me years ago. He drove my brother so far underground that I've never been able to find him. And he didn't even give me a chance to say goodbye before he died. You think a letter will bother me?''

He looked up at the ceiling then, his voice harsh with grief. "Well, to hell with you, Sam Gallagher—you hear me, wherever you are? You're gone and I'm here, and I'll be damned if I'll spend one more minute caring."

Then he looked down at Maddie. "So you just tell me what he could have said that would give me a second's pause. I don't think you know me well enough to know what I can take." His eyes turned cold—colder than the light from a distant star and every bit as lonely.

"Boone—" She reached out and placed her hand on his muscular forearm. The contact shocked them both—she could see it in the quick flare in his eyes, could feel it all the way down her spine. "It's not anything like what you're thinking, but it won't make you feel any better."

A muscle jumped in his rock-hard jaw. He pulled his arm away, and Maddie felt the loss.

In a voice deceptively soft, he asked, "Why don't you let me be the judge of that?"

So be it. "All right." Maddie drew a deep breath, wishing she had stayed out on the porch. She lifted her gaze and met his squarely. "He said that he was afraid to find Dalton or to tell Jenny that Dalton was alive."

Boone's hard expression didn't flicker. "Why would he be afraid?"

Maddie swallowed. "Because your mother loved my father first, and Sam was afraid he would lose her."

Boone still didn't move and his gaze never wavered. Behind him, Vondell gasped in disbelief.

His voice betrayed nothing of his feelings. "I'd like to read the letter."

"Are you sure?"

Boone nodded, his laugh short and rusty. "Yeah." But his eyes told a different story. "I'm sure."

"Boone, I'm sorry. I don't know what—"

"Just get the letter, Maddie."

She traded sympathetic glances with Vondell, then ran up to her room and got Sam's letter. Back in the kitchen, she handed it to Boone. She stayed quiet, though she could have recited every word after all the hours she'd spent trying to decide if any of it was real.

Dear Maddie Rose,

I was hoping we'd get to meet, but the doc says it's not likely. In any case, my lawyer will be contacting you with this letter and the provisions of my will. You don't know me, but my name is Sam Gallagher and your father was once my best friend. I wronged your father, Maddie Rose, but it's too late to make it right with him, so I'm giving you the house that should have been his.

It probably comes as a surprise to hear that I'm leaving you a ranch house in Texas. This house belonged to your grandmother Rose and was the place where your father grew up. It should have been his when Rose died, but by then everyone believed he was dead. I bought it from Rose's estate, not knowing until a few years later that Dalton was alive.

That's why I'm leaving it to you, Maddie—because I should have looked for Dalton then, and I didn't. You see, my Jenny loved Dalton first, and I was afraid I'd lose her. I know she only married me because Dalton was gone. By the time I found out he was alive, we had our two boys, Mitch and Boone, and we'd built a good life together. But there was always this sadness in Jenny, and I knew it was because she lost Dalton.

A few years after I bought this place, my Jenny passed away. I never got over her, never loved another woman. Gallagher men love only once, you see. But I should have trusted Jenny and told her about Dalton. I'd like to believe she would have stayed with me, but I couldn't take the chance.

If you don't want the place, that's fine. The land will go to my sons and it won't go down easy with Boone, especially, for you to have the house. But give yourself a chance to love the place as your daddy did. I'm making it a condition that you stay in the house for thirty days before you make up your mind. It might take a while to grow on you.

I hope you and my sons can make peace with what I've done. At the end of the thirty days, if you don't want the house, I want you to sell it to Boone. I think he'll want it, now that he won't have to put up with me. But if you decide to stay, there's plenty of land for them to build their own houses on. It's as fair as I know how to be.

I hear that you're a fancy cook back east, but Devlin also tells me you have no other family. Your blood runs deep in this place, Maddie Rose. You have roots here. Generations of Wheelers fought and died, battled drought and Indians and heartache to keep this place. I believe old Rose would like knowing you were here.

I was off in the service when everything went bad for Dalton, but I know he would have hated to leave. People think he killed his stepfather, but he didn't. He confessed and then vanished to save his mother from the consequences of what she'd done. In my heart, I know he never felt at home anywhere else, and she never stopped missing him.

Give it a chance, Maddie Rose. See if Texas whispers in your heart the way it always has in mine. This house was a happy place once, when Jenny was here, but it hasn't been happy in years. See if you can bring it back to life.

Sam Gallagher

When Boone finished, he stared at her for a long, long moment. Then his voice came, so low she almost couldn't hear it.

"You can't mean to stay." His voice was firm, but those eyes...

"No," she whispered back. "I won't be staying."

Boone laid the letter down on the old scarred table. Then he pushed past Maddie, leaving the air stinging with anguish so deep that it echoed in the room. The back door slammed behind him, and Maddie could only stand very still.

Vondell crossed over and picked up the letter, reading it slowly. Then she heaved a big sigh and pressed one set of fingers to her forehead. "Curse you, Sam Gallagher. It never had to be like this."

Maddie's chest ached. "I said I was going. If I could leave right now, I would, Vondell." She lifted her gaze to see the older woman's grim visage. "I won't stay a minute longer than I must. But surely he's not so mad that he would want to lose the whole place just to get me out of here."

"He's not mad at you, child. He's just got a hurt real deep—so deep it's never healed. Boone's a proud man, too proud to admit it. He was proud even as a young man, and he'd take a bullet before he'd admit how much he wanted his father to love him. The only happy memories Boone has of this place are from when Jenny was still alive. Hearing that Jenny loved a man we all thought was a murderer was bound to go down hard."

"I tried to warn him."

"In some ways, Boone's as hardheaded as Sam."

"I won't make this any harder for him than I have to, Vondell, but I am not hiding in my room for a month."

"Of course you shouldn't." Vondell patted her arm and smiled. "Sam was right about one thing—this old place needs someone to liven it up. I'm thinking you're just the person for the job. You just be yourself, Maddie girl. No harm in that."

Maddie's laugh was shakier than she'd have liked. "I doubt that Boone would agree."

"Well, maybe Boone Gallagher needs a little shaking up. Heaven knows this place has held little enough happiness since Jenny died." She smiled more brightly. "Now how about you show me what magic you can make from a carrot?"

Maddie had to smile back. Thank heavens Vondell was here.

And that come tomorrow it would be only twenty-eight days and counting.

Boone climbed the stairs and headed down the hall, years of practice dispensing with the need for lights. The house was quiet. He'd heard Vondell's soft snores downstairs, and he saw no light from under Maddie's door.

He paused outside her door, remembering the look on her face when he'd finished Sam's letter. She had a soft heart—too soft to be caught in Sam's games. He no longer believed that she was anything more than an innocent victim, a pawn caught in the swirling winds of long-ago disasters. But that didn't mean he could let down his guard. Her sheer attractiveness was reason enough, never mind the potential damage she could do if she wanted to.

He couldn't afford to run her off before her thirty days was up, and because of that, he appreciated the stubborn streak that ran a mile wide down her back. He also couldn't risk her learning to like this place and deciding to stay.

Not that it seemed much of a risk, Boone thought as he opened the door to his room. The picture beside his bed kept that fresh in his mind. Helen's blond perfection shone out at him—the Helen he'd first met, not the one he'd last seen.

She'd hated it here, and so would Maddie. As soon as the newness wore off, the restlessness would set in. Boone would have to tread a fine line; his best course was to keep an eye out, but stay far, far away. Maddie might hold temptation for him, but she also had the potential to cost him the only thing he had left.

Vondell could keep her entertained when she started to go stir-crazy, wanting out of this place.

People thought Boone kept Helen's picture out because he was still mourning. They couldn't be farther off the mark.

He kept the picture there to remind him. His father had gone wrong, loving too much. Boone had gone wrong, loving too little. He would avoid both paths to tragedy.

No more love. No more city girls. No more mistakes.

## Chapter Four

"Would you look at that?" Jim Caskey whistled.

Boone glanced up from cleaning Gulliver's hoof. The minute he did, he wished he hadn't.

"I didn't know a body would bend that way," Jim observed.

Jim's horse shifted, and Gulliver got edgy.

"Pay attention, Jim."

"Oh, I am, Boone. I surely am."

"To your horse," Boone clarified.

"Don't tell me that sight don't get your mind working. Any woman that limber—"

"Can it, Jim. Velda would skin and gut you."

"She would, at that. But it might be worth it."

Boone took another look and wished he hadn't. The skintight leotard Maddie wore only emphasized the long legs, the lush breasts, the waist he knew he could span with his hands—

Damn it. He didn't want to notice, had tried to forget she existed. He'd stayed gone from sunup to past supper for three days, avoiding her.

"Whew, Boone, you see that?" Sonny Chavez rounded the corner.

"He sees, all right. He just ain't admittin' it," Jim replied.

"Don't you two have anything better to do? If not, maybe this ranch needs to cut the payroll some."

The two muttered a little, then started moving away, chuckling at something Jim had said. Boone ignored them and concentrated on the hoof pick he wielded, noting that it was past time for Gulliver to be shod.

He let the hoof down and picked up the last one, making short work of cleaning it, studiously ignoring the movement on the porch. But when he let down the last hoof, the gelding shifted and grazed the side of Boone's foot. Twelve-hundred pounds, even at a glancing blow, hurt like hell.

"Ouch—damn it!"

Laughter erupted from the doorway. Boone shot a glare where Jim and Sonny stood. "You might want to mind your own advice," Jim chided. Then he disappeared around the corner.

That did it. Boone chucked the hoof pick into a bucket and started walking, his temper flaring with every step.

It didn't help that she was so graceful, that the limber, elegant movements were almost poetry in motion. Maddie had no business doing whatever that was right here, in full view of the men. Didn't the woman have a shred of modesty?

Of course she didn't. Boone only had to remember the slip of a dress she'd worn the day she came, or the scrap of lace he'd seen in the window. Never mind that millions of women wore much less. Of course, he'd seen Maddie in an old baggy T-shirt yesterday and even that seemed to look—

Hell.

Seductive. It wasn't the clothes. It was the clothes on *her*.

Twenty-six days and counting.

"What the hell do you think you're doing?" he barked.

Maddie jolted, but drew in a deep breath and maintained the stance she held. She looked like a human pretzel. Like Jim, he never realized the body could do things like that.

"I *was* relaxing and doing my yoga," she replied. "I'll continue if you'd leave me alone."

"Why do you have to do it out here?"

Slowly, she untwisted her body and centered her torso over legs spread impossibly wide. Then she bent over in the center, facing him, resting her elbows on the ground.

Boone gritted his teeth and tried not to notice the lean muscles of her thighs, the smooth, tight—

"I asked you a question. Why can't you do this in your room?"

As slowly as before, Maddie unbent from the waist, her torso rising and giving him a clear view of cleavage he didn't want to see. Her head lifted, and those bewitching gray eyes studied him too closely.

He wanted to look away. So he didn't.

"You're a perfect candidate for yoga, Boone. You need to relax worse than anyone I ever met."

"I'll relax when—" He forced himself to stop.

One dark eyebrow arched. "When I'm gone?"

"I've got work to do. Find some other place to do that stuff. Some place where you don't distract the men." He turned to walk away.

"Yoga does wonders to clear the mind and cleanse the soul. I could teach you."

He turned back around. "I'm not the one on vacation. I don't have time to play games."

"It's not a game." Suddenly she looked very serious. "I couldn't have made it through the last year without it."

"Cooking little appetizers is such hard work?"

She smiled. "As a matter of fact, it is, but that's not what I'm talking about. Yoga is as much a mental discipline as it is physical. But it's something more. It's a way to refresh the soul, to touch a part of life we forget to experience."

Boone sensed that there was more to the story. For one second, he thought about asking what it was that she had needed to make it through. Then he reminded himself that she was only temporary. The last thing he needed was to get involved in her problems. He had enough of his own.

"You could use a break, Boone." Her gray eyes went soft, the pale centers seeing too much. "You work too hard."

Sometimes he felt as though he'd been tired for years. At that moment, he felt the call of her gentleness, a brief instant of longing for the spark of whatever it was that made Maddie more vivacious than any woman he'd ever met.

And because he did, he shoved it away with harsh words. "That's something I'd expect from a city girl. Work on a ranch is never done. Seven days a week, the animals need tending. We don't get vacation or sick leave."

"Everyone needs some downtime, Boone."

"Sam let this place go too much when he was sick. I've got a lot to do to bring it back." He couldn't afford to buy her out if he didn't get things back running smoothly.

And he would buy her out. He'd never let the Caswells have this place, not while there was breath left in his body.

"Finish your contortions, Maddie Rose, and quit distracting my men." Boone's voice went harsh, and he saw it reflected in her eyes.

She leaned down and picked up the purple mat she'd been using. "What time do the men get to work?" Her voice was so quiet that he could barely hear her.

"They're here by seven."

Maddie shot him a look that covered hurt with challenge. "My room is too small. I like the view and the clean air. I'll be finished before they arrive." Back straight as an arrow, slender limbs moving with a grace he couldn't help but admire, Maddie walked across the porch and went inside.

That would take care of the men and their roving eyes.

Now if only Boone could take care of his own.

Maddie couldn't get enough of mornings. Always a night owl before, she found that mornings here tugged at her, called out a song she didn't want to miss.

And the garden. Was there ever such a luxury as getting dirt under your fingernails? Would she ever have believed she'd say that?

And wouldn't Robert shudder? The very thought made Maddie smile. Opening the gate to Vondell's garden, Maddie stepped inside, bucket in hand, as eager as if she'd opened Aladdin's cave.

Tomatoes. She'd start there. *No, Maddie. Save them for last. They bruise—they have to go on top.*

But she snatched a cherry tomato off the vine as she passed and popped it straight into her mouth, the flavor exploding inside, drenching her taste buds with rich, luscious tang.

She laughed, imagining Robert reeling in horror that she hadn't even washed it first. *You're so impulsive, Maddie.*

Yes, she was. And she loved it.

Soon she squatted between rows of bush beans, carefully judging readiness, snapping off only those exactly ripe, already wondering if she could convince Vondell to let her cook tonight. She'd been too long away from her kitchen. Radish roses just weren't enough. Maybe Vondell would like a vacation.

Then she heard Boone's voice, soft and gentle, sounding as she'd never before heard it. It had to be a woman he wooed with that voice; it would certainly woo her. This was another Boone she'd never met.

She peered up over the bushes to see who the lucky woman was. And then she bit down on her lip to stifle a laugh.

Or maybe a sigh. God, he looked good.

Over his jeans, Boone wore leather chaps. They showcased parts of his anatomy in a way that should have been outlawed.

But it wasn't just Boone's very impressive anatomy that caught her attention. It was his manner with the colt.

Maddie knew nothing about horses, but she guessed that this one would grow into an impressive specimen. Right now, though, he was still shorter than Boone. Inside the round pen, the colt stood very still, while Boone ran his hands over the horse's entire body, talking to him all the time.

It was amazing. The horse acted part dog, part cat, eagerly luxuriating at the touch of Boone's strong, gentle hands. Sometimes the colt would almost seem to lean toward Boone as if begging for more.

Boone smiled. Boone laughed. He moved and talked, praised and caressed, strong and in command, but never misusing the strength.

And Maddie couldn't help but wonder how much it mirrored the way Boone would make love.

*You'll never find out, so just stop wondering.* Even if Boone had given her a single sign of welcome, the idea was futile. She'd already seen enough of Boone to know that he took life very seriously. Even if he would indulge in a meaningless fling, instinct told her that he would never do it here at the ranch. And that's all it could be, a fling, a temporary affair. She would be gone in just a few weeks.

Besides, Maddie herself wasn't the type for casual sex. Hot, yes—oh, yes. Meaningless, no. She led with her heart, no matter how she had tried to change. It was the reason she'd sworn off men for the foreseeable future.

Part of the reason she'd come to Texas had been to take a hiatus from men. Cowboys weren't her type, and she'd expected to confront no temptations.

But Boone was not an easy man to ignore. A new layer emerged every time she was around him. Good looks, she could forget—New York was full of good-looking men. But Boone was full of contrasts—rugged but gentle, hard but haunted, a man whose rough edges were proving to hide surprising pockets of tenderness.

Except around her, of course.

It didn't matter. She would be gone soon. Maddie turned back to the green beans, concentrating so fiercely that she started at the voice behind her.

"Ma'am?"

Maddie almost lost her balance. She rose to face the man she'd been told was the foreman. "Yes?"

Fiftyish and tanned from long hours in the sun, the man grinned a craggy smile. "I'm Jim Caskey, ma'am. I'm the foreman around here."

"I'm Maddie Collins. Pleased to meet you."

"Same here." He shifted on his feet but didn't speak again. He studied the ground.

"Is there something you need, Mr. Caskey?"

His head jerked up. "What? Oh—no, no. Nice day, don't you think?"

Maddie resisted the urge to laugh. One of the hardest things to get used to was the pace of life around here. Conversations moved as slowly as everything else. But she was learning. She scanned the sky. "Yes, it is. Hot, though."

He looked relieved, like they'd discovered a common language. "Don't think it'll rain. Prob'ly tonight, though. My knee always knows."

"Your knee?"

"Yes, ma'am. I got this trick knee from when I rode bulls and it's better than that radar they got over in Abilene."

"Really?" She pinched her thigh so the pain would keep her face straight. "It never misses?"

He shook his head. "Purt' near perfect record."

"Wow. That's amazing." They stood in silence

for a long moment. "Can I help you with something, Mr. Caskey?"

"Please call me Jim, ma'am. Mr. Caskey's my dad."

"Okay—Jim. Do you think you could call me Maddie? 'Ma'am' makes me feel like I could be your mother."

His face creased in a wide grin, his eyes sparkling. "Oh, trust me, ma'am—uh, Maddie. My mother never looked anything like you. Fact is, me and Sonny, we can't help noticin'—"

"Sonny is the other gentleman who works with you?"

"Yes, ma'am—uh, Maddie. But he's married, too." Jim's eyes lost their sparkle. "I mean, his wife's real nice and all, just that you should know—"

Maddie wasn't sure how much longer she could keep her face straight. If there was a point to this conversation, she wondered if they'd reach it today. "I understand, Jim. I'll try to keep my hands to myself."

The man looked honestly horrified. "Oh, I never meant that you would—" His face went redder than the tomatoes beside her. He cleared his throat. "Actually, it's just that I noticed—well, me and Sonny noticed that you sure seem to like this garden. Seems odd for a city girl."

Maddie resisted a sigh of frustration. "It's a treat to take food straight off the plant instead of the grocery shelves."

"Well, my Velda's got peach trees, and I brought you some of her peaches, if you think you'd like them. But if you don't, that's all right."

"Fresh peaches?" Maddie's heart thumped.

"Picked this morning."

"Oh, Jim, that's wonderful!" Maddie hugged a fistful of beans to her breast. "I may faint from pleasure."

He shifted his weight from one foot to the other. "Aw, please don't do that. I'd have to catch you and then Boone would get all mad and Velda would skin and gut me. It wouldn't hardly be worth it."

Maddie did laugh then. "Velda is your wife?"

"Thirty-four years."

"That's wonderful. How romantic."

"Well, now." He shuffled again. "Velda don't think I'm very romantic."

"Staying with the same woman for thirty-four years sounds pretty romantic to me, Jim. Especially since your voice tells me you love her."

He reddened once more. "Well, I, uh—sure I do." Then he glanced up, assessing. "You're not like Helen at all."

"Helen?"

"Boone's wife."

Maddie couldn't contain her shock. "Boone has a wife?"

"She's dead. Died a couple of years back."

"I'm so sorry." That explained the shadows. "Boone must have been devastated."

Jim's voice went flat. "He was. But she hated this place."

Maddie frowned.

"She was a fancy woman, a city girl like you. But she never tried to like it. Between her and Sam, they made Boone's life hell."

"What happened to her?"

Jim's eyes narrowed, his jaw hard. "She drowned."

"Oh, I'm so sorry."

"Don't be. She was—" He looked distinctly uncomfortable. "It's not really my story to tell, Maddie."

She wished it were. "I understand. So that's why Boone doesn't like city girls? Because his wife was miserable here?"

Jim cut a glance over toward Boone. "Don't get the wrong idea. There's more to it than that. But I've already said too much."

"That's all right, Jim. And I don't hold it against him. He came back home to find that a stranger has inherited the house that should be his. We're both in an awkward position. A few more weeks, and then both of us can get back to our lives."

"You wouldn't consider staying?"

Maddie smiled gently. "It's lovely here. Not like anything I'm used to, but it has its own charm. But my life is…different from this."

"I imagine so. You sure brighten a place up, though."

Maddie smiled, her heart warmed. "That's the nicest thing anyone's said to me in a long time."

His face grew serious. "Don't think badly of Boone, Maddie. He's had a hard go of it. Truth to tell, I'm not sure I would have ever come back— not after what he went through the last time he was here." He glanced over at Boone and the colt. "But he belongs here. I never saw a man who could handle a horse better. This place needs him, and he needs to be here."

Maddie smiled fondly. "Boone's lucky to have a friend like you."

"Well." Jim shifted his hat in his hand. Maddie studied the line on his forehead where his tan ended. "I'll just get those peaches for you and leave them with Vondell. Best get to work." He settled his hat back on his head and turned to leave.

"Jim?"

Jim turned back.

"Thank you."

"I'll tell Velda."

"Please do, but I'm thanking you for making me feel welcome."

Once again, his face turned red and he ducked his head slightly. "You're welcome. Stick around a while, Maddie. The place might grow on you."

"I don't think Boone would like that much."

"Aw, hell—I mean heck, Maddie. Boone ain't the only one around here. You spruce up the place real nicely, if you ask me."

Maddie laughed, charmed to her toes. "Well, I'll just keep sprucin' then."

He tipped his hat. "You do that, Maddie. You just do that."

Maddie watched him go. This place might be short on amenities, but the people were a marvel: plain, honest, simple people who said what they thought and didn't play mind games.

Well, Boone wasn't plain and he sure wasn't simple, but she understood his reaction better now. He was wrong about her, but it didn't matter. She didn't have to see him much with Vondell as a buffer.

Maddie finished up quickly, then headed into the house, already savoring her peaches. "Vondell? Did Jim—?"

Vondell turned, one hand clapped over her ear so she could hear the phone better. Her face was pinched and dead white. "All right," she said into the receiver. "I'll get there as soon as I can." She hung up slowly.

"What is it? What's the matter?"

"It's my sister. She fell and broke her hip."

"I'm so sorry."

"Maddie, I don't like leaving you like this, but my sister has no one else. I have to go stay with her for a few weeks until she can get around on her own again."

Maddie faltered a minute, but recovered quickly. "Of course you do. What can I do to help you?"

"Will you be all right here? You don't have to

cook or anything. Boone can get his own meals, I expect.''

Maddie walked over and gave the smaller woman a hug. ''Don't you worry about us, Vondell. I was about to ask you if I could cook tonight. I'm afraid my knife hand is itching to get back to work. I've never been much on sitting around.''

''Lordy, child, I hate to go now, with so much unsettled between you and Boone.''

Maddie hoped that she sounded more convincing than she felt. ''Vondell, this is the nineties. It's a very big house. Boone and I don't need a chaperone—and I'll do my best to see that we don't need a referee. If we do, maybe Jim will do the honors.''

Vondell smiled faintly, but her brow furrowed again all too quickly. ''My sister's health hasn't been good lately.''

Maddie put her arm around the older woman and ushered her down the hall to her room. ''You just concentrate on your sister. If it will make you feel better, give me the phone number and I'll promise to call you before I slam a frying pan into Boone's thick head.''

Vondell laughed then, her old cackle. ''Oh, child, I might ask you to wait so I could watch that.'' She sobered. ''You don't have to be afraid of Boone, you know. He's got a good heart. It's just been abused.''

''I believe that. I'm truly not worried. Besides, he works all day outside, and I'll be in here. We'll hardly see each other. We'll do fine.''

Vondell turned back to her and studied her carefully. "I hope so. I surely hope so."

"Believe it," Maddie insisted. "Piece of cake."

She resisted the urge to cross her fingers behind her back.

An hour later, Boone and Maddie stood on the porch, waving goodbye to Vondell. When her car disappeared from sight, Boone slapped his hat against his jeans' leg. "Well, guess I'll be getting back to work. Don't worry about cooking for me, no matter what Vondell asked. I've been taking care of myself for a long time."

"You're not afraid to be alone with me, are you, Boone?" Maddie's eyes glowed silver. He couldn't decide if it was mischief or worry.

He studied her slowly. "No reason to be, is there?" But he knew there was. From where he stood, he could smell her: the rich, mysterious scent that wafted through his dreams all too often.

"I can't waste any more time standing here." He clapped his hat back on his head. "I've got work to do."

Behind him, he heard Maddie's exhaled frustration. He was being hard on her, but he had his reasons.

It was damn foolish, but somehow even knowing that Maddie's bed lay only thirty feet or so from his every night, Vondell's presence downstairs had provided a barrier. Now Vondell was gone, and the nights would get a whole lot longer.

He wished he could forget the feel of Maddie's body, wished he could banish the images that crowded in—Maddie smiling and laughing, carrying on with Vondell, teasing Jim. Checking on that calf every day like it was her pet dog, for Pete's sake.

Maddie was sexy, there was no doubt about it. That voice seemed to crawl down his spine and settle deep into his gut every time he heard it. But it was Maddie's spirit that was far more dangerous to him.

She breathed life into this old place, just like Sam had wanted, damn him. And in a few weeks, she would leave and take the sparkle with her. A fast round of hot sex would relieve some of the pressure for the moment, but it would only make things worse in the long run.

Boone already felt in his bones that if he ever got his hands on Maddie, once would never be enough.

And now their chaperone was gone. The ranch hands left at night, too.

This house was big, all right.

But not big enough for him to forget that Maddie was in it with him.

## Chapter Five

Boone stopped on the back porch for a minute, rolling his left shoulder and cursing the mare. Dancer got more fractious by the day. She was new since he'd last been on the ranch, but everything told him her labor wouldn't be easy. He'd have to watch her closely.

It had been a long day. He'd slap a sandwich together and try not to miss Vondell's cooking too much—

But the minute he opened the kitchen door, something smelled so good that Boone's mouth started watering.

Then his gaze lit on Maddie, and he almost groaned out loud.

She looked right at home. And she looked good, damn it.

Her dark hair was piled haphazardly on her head, anchored by what looked like chopsticks that shimmied gently as she turned. "Hi. Ready to eat?" Maddie smiled.

"I told you not to cook for me."

"No, you told me I didn't *have* to cook for you. I miss cooking. Gotta keep my knife hand sharp."

The sparkle in her eyes, the mischief in her grin—both drew him like a beacon.

As if ignoring her presence in the night ahead wasn't already going to be tough enough.

He should get started ignoring her now—but man, did something smell good.

Her smile widened. "No radish roses, I promise."

Boone couldn't help his own grin. "Don't tell me—tofu burgers instead."

Maddie's laugh started out pure and clear like a bell, then slid down the scale to a low, sultry chuckle. For a moment, all Boone could do was stare. Escaping tendrils of her hair curled around a face flushed from the stove's heat, and she had a smudge of flour on one cheek. She wore old cutoff jeans and another one of those damn too-short tops that exposed the smooth skin of her midriff. One of Vondell's aprons was wrapped around that sweet patch of skin right now—but Boone knew it was there.

And his fingers wanted to touch it.

Badly.

Just one slow slide of fingertips across satin. It *would* be satin, he was sure of it.

"I'm happy to know you're interested," she said.

His body responded so fast that Boone almost got whiplash, jerking his head up. "You—are?" he croaked.

"I like tofu burgers. I make great ones."

Damn. Close call. She would know his thoughts if he didn't get control, quickly.

Then he looked more closely. Within that sparkle of mischief, the sure instinct of a woman gleamed. Her pupils went dark in silent response to him.

It was already too late. She knew.

His gaze slid down to those lips that drove him crazy. His hands flexed, fingers ready to slide beneath that apron.

Maybe it wouldn't hurt anything. Maybe they could—

*No.* The old prickling warning stopped him. Nothing would be simple or easy with Maddie. He would want more than one roll in the hay with this woman.

Boone tore his gaze away and stared toward the hall, clearing a throat gone suddenly parched. "I've got horse and sweat all over me. Do I have time to shower?"

He risked one glance at Maddie. The smooth skin above her bodice flushed rosy. Her lips were slightly parted, and the mischief had fled from her eyes. He saw a different Maddie—unsteady and vulnerable, not her usual cheerful, indomitable self. Boone realized he'd come to expect Maddie to always rise to the challenge, to stay unflappable in her own flaky way.

He didn't like knowing that he'd caused this. Not when there was no future in pursuing it.

Oh, he'd like to rattle Maddie, big time. He'd like to shake the foundations of her world. Drown himself in making love to her and pull her into the whirlpool with him.

But Maddie didn't belong here. She wouldn't stay.

And he wasn't leaving this place again. Couldn't afford to have it haunted any more than it already was.

Almost a whisper, her answer drifted to him in that damn husky voice. "Ten minutes enough?"

Boone felt the sting of wry amusement, but he didn't grin. Ten *years* wouldn't be enough.

"Ten minutes, it is." Boone made a grateful escape.

*He wanted her.*

Maddie stared across the now-empty kitchen, her mind reeling like a drunk in search of the next bottle.

Then her common sense took over.

Boone might want her, but he didn't like her. Robert had once wanted her, too. Had praised her, turned her head with compliments, made her feel unique and special. At first.

But it had been as much because he'd needed her and the flair he had praised—for the success of the restaurant. Maddie knew now that she had been the magic ingredient that had packed the place every night. It wasn't arrogant to admit that—she'd had many reports that the restaurant stood half empty most nights now. The patrons apparently missed both her cooking and the visits she made to the tables. Maddie loved feeding people, listening to them, keeping up with their families. Making them her family.

It was pathetic how long it had taken Maddie to realize that exactly the color and flair that made her a prized chef had been what Robert had tried to stamp out of her when the restaurant doors were closed. As if she should have some off-on switch like he had—all charm and grace during working hours, but all Boston propriety the rest of the time.

Boone needed Maddie, too. To keep his ranch intact.

But he didn't approve of her, didn't like who she was, didn't believe she belonged here. No amount of pleasure, no amount of wondering how those strong hands would feel all over her body, was worth having to recover her sense of herself again.

She didn't have an off-on switch. She was who she was, and she had no one else now. If Maddie let anyone destroy her faith in herself again, she didn't know if she could rebuild it this time.

Boone tempted her, all right. A lot. Something about him called to her, and it wasn't just a set of impressive muscles or a handsome face.

But he didn't want her here—not permanently. It was right that he should have this house that meant so much to him, but Maddie already thought that she might want to come back, just to visit. There was something about this place that pulled at her, despite knowing that she would never truly fit.

If she and Boone could be friends, she could come back to visit, maybe. He would marry and have children, sure—make this house the home that he remembered from happier times. She could be friends with his wife, bring presents to his kids.

*If* they were friends. Only friends and nothing more.

The crackle of butter close to burning yanked Maddie back. *Just cook, Maddie. Get through dinner. Then go take your walk and get away from him. With any luck, he'll be in bed before you return.*

Boone drained his glass of ice water and got up to refill it.

''Thanks. I can't leave this right now.'' Maddie spoke to him, but her gaze was firmly fixed on the stove.

''This isn't your restaurant. You don't have to give me good service. I've been taking care of myself for a long time now.''

She did glance up at him then. ''I guess old habits are hard to break. I waited tables for a long time while I was learning the business.'' The mischief rose again. ''I made good money on tips.''

He grinned back. ''Whoever had you waiting tables instead of making the food was a fool. That smells great.''

Delight brightened her eyes. ''You haven't tried it yet.''

''Need a taster?''

For just a second, he could swear he saw nerves fracture the delight. Then she wiped her hands on her apron and reached into a nearby drawer for a spoon. Scooping up sauce, she blew across the spoon before lifting it to his mouth. Boone couldn't take his gaze from her lips.

When he didn't respond quickly enough to the raised spoon, Maddie looked up at him. Their gazes slid together, and Boone felt his breath lock up in his chest.

She was so close. All he had to do was reach out and touch the flesh that his hands still remembered.

Maddie's breasts rose with her quick inhalation. Her nostrils flared. Those eerie silvery eyes went dark, and Boone knew all he had to do was take the next step. She was as aware of him as he was of her.

And she wasn't stepping away.

He could kiss those lips. He could taste her on his tongue. He could lick a slow, soft trail down the slender line of her throat, sip the salty dew from her body—

The oven buzzer went off, and jolted them both.

Boone gripped his glass so hard that it was a miracle it didn't break.

''I'll wait for the meal.'' He turned away, grasping for control, hearing his voice crack as it hadn't done since adolescence. As fast as he could, he put kitchen floor between them.

This was never going to work. They were oil and water. Maddie was meant for bright lights and center stage. He only wanted the horses, the big sky, the quiet.

She was going to leave, and he would stay.

The barn was full, but maybe he should make room in the tack room. Or the back of his truck. Or anywhere but locked in this house with Maddie.

Twenty-six days and counting.

When she set the food on the table, Boone couldn't stifle his amazement at the simple fare. Linguine with marinara sauce. Salad. Garlic bread, hot from the oven.

His amazement must have shown.

"I told you—no radish roses."

Boone glanced up. Nerves and something darker danced in her eyes, but she held her head high and proud as if daring him to say anything about what had happened.

"I figured it would still be something fancy."

"Taste it. I told you, good food is good food."

So he did. And it was the best thing he'd put in his mouth in ages. Vondell was a good cook, but this sauce held a world of flavors—robust and teasing on his tongue. He took a bite of the bread and almost sighed out loud.

He realized Maddie wasn't eating—just watching him. "You're not going to eat?"

"I will, but right now I'm just enjoying seeing someone eat my food again. It's what I do. I feed people."

"I can't imagine why anyone ever let you leave

New York. This is the best marinara I've ever tasted.''

Surprise and delight jousted for top billing. ''You know it's marinara?''

Boone had to smile. ''I've traveled a lot of places. And people in Texas know what marinara is, Maddie.'' He shook his head. ''Well, Jim probably doesn't, but—''

Maddie laughed then, and Boone let the sound of it wash over him like a river's bounty in the heat of summer. For a moment, he wanted to stop time, to simply enjoy the moment—the food, the laughter, the woman. To let it cleanse away the layers of hard feelings that time had painted into the corners of every room of this house.

For just a moment, Boone could feel what it had been like when his mother was alive, when this house had last rung with laughter.

''Did your wife like to cook?''

Boone froze. ''Who talked to you about Helen?''

''No one talked to me about her—not really. Jim just mentioned...I'm sorry. I know she died. It must have been very hard on you. If you don't want to talk about her—''

''I don't.''

''I see.'' She went solemn. ''I'm sorry.''

''You don't see, but it doesn't matter.'' He'd known better than to let down his guard. ''We don't need to know each other's life stories. No point in it.''

Maddie laid down her fork and drew a deep

breath, straightening her shoulders. All the fun had vanished from her eyes. Slowly she rose and carried her untouched plate to the counter, removing her apron.

"It's time for my walk. Just leave the kitchen, and I'll clean it up when I get back." A tiny tremor threaded through her voice as her lips curved faintly at the corners. "They say the best chefs make the biggest messes. It's pretty obvious I'm a great chef."

Then she left, her gait stiff as if she were holding herself together. She headed out the front door and down the hill, as was her nightly habit.

Boone stared at his plate and wondered if he ought to just go kick a puppy for good measure.

After cleaning the kitchen, Boone walked out onto the front porch and sat on the steps in the dwindling twilight. He didn't see Maddie on the road anywhere, but her car was still here so she couldn't have gone far.

He scanned the vista before him, his gaze, as always, wandering toward the little pioneer cemetery down the hill on a piece of their land. Coyote Valley Cemetery held the bones of those who had settled this place, had carved out lives from a harsh, unwelcoming land.

His mother was buried there, as was Rose Wheeler. Sam would be there, too, but Boone hadn't paid a visit yet. He knew the reckoning was out there in the future—that someday, somehow, he had to figure out a way to let the past go. For now, he had more to do than he could say grace over. Maybe once he'd scraped together the money and bought Maddie out, once the whole place was his again and he'd found Mitch, he could start to forgive his father.

But right now that day seemed very far away. The days between now and when Maddie left were all he could handle.

He thought about his brother, and about the phone conversation he'd had with Devlin Marlowe. Marlowe seemed to have his head on straight and know what he was doing. He'd said he might pay a visit and see if he could find anything left in Sam's papers that might help him get closer to Mitch's trail.

Boone had told him to hold off for a day or so. He wanted to find his brother, but now the house belonged to Maddie. Boone felt obligated to clear it with her, even though nothing of Sam's was likely to mean anything to her.

And before he did that, he had an apology to make. Her question about Helen had seemed motivated by honest curiosity. He couldn't even be sure that she'd heard anything about the circumstances…and no one on this place knew the whole story anyway.

What he had said was true. They didn't need to know each other's life stories. They only had to co-exist for a few more weeks; then they'd never see one another again.

And while that idea turned his thoughts somber, it was a fact. It was real. Boone had learned long ago not to moon over what couldn't be.

But even though it was real and inescapable that the less each knew about the other, the better off they'd be, Boone wasn't in the habit of kicking puppies: he'd been rough with Maddie when she didn't deserve it, and he would apologize. Cleaning up the kitchen was a start, but, like most women, Maddie would appreciate the words.

A movement down the hill caught his eye. Maddie had been in the cemetery. He wondered why.

*Your blood runs deep in this place, Maddie Rose. You have roots here.*

The words from Sam's letter sent a chill through Boone's blood.

He hoped Maddie wouldn't get romantic about this and make things more complicated than they already were.

Boone thought about going on to bed and talking to Maddie tomorrow. He shook his head and pulled out his knife, spying a broken tree branch lying on the ground. Picking it up, he turned to the whittling that had always helped him think.

He'd just sit here and whittle while he waited for her return. He'd apologize. Then he'd go to bed, get a good night's sleep, and do his damnedest to keep the ranch going, come up with the money, and pretend Maddie Rose was invisible.

*Sure thing, Boone. Maybe you should save that money and buy yourself that bridge in the desert— easier deal, all the way around.*

Maddie walked back up the hill, her mind awhirl. She shouldn't have gone into the little cemetery.

She'd barely regained her calm and her determination to keep things in perspective, remembered that this was not her home, that she couldn't get romantic about cooking in her grandmother's kitchen. Boone was right, more right than he knew. She had plenty in her own life that she didn't want to discuss, and her foolish fancies of being Boone's friend and coming back to visit were just that—fantasies.

Then she'd decided to see inside the little cemetery, where tall juniper sentinels guarded the departed so securely. She wasn't a person who was spooked easily, and cemeteries had never bothered her before. She didn't fear ghosts or spirits walking the night.

But this cemetery had done something she'd never expected: it had charmed her. Among the junipers was an almost palpable sense of peace…and history. The historical marker at the entrance noted that only members of pioneer families were buried there. She'd gone looking for Rose Wheeler's grave.

Somehow she hadn't been prepared for the feeling of looking at the simple headstone and knowing that her grandmother's bones rested there, cradled in the earth where Maddie stood. For the first time, it all seemed real. A sense of connection had pulled at her, and Maddie was shaken by it still.

Her grandmother. Maddie wanted to talk to someone who had known her. With a hunger that swept through her like a blast furnace, Maddie suddenly wanted to know what her grandmother looked like, how she laughed, how her voice sounded, what she wore.

And it didn't matter that she wouldn't stay here, that she couldn't stay here, that her life was elsewhere. Maddie wanted to take her heritage with her, wherever she landed. So she had made a promise, then and there, that she would make it her mission to find out as much as she could, in these weeks, about the people she came from. She wasn't a person to lie around, anyway, and if Boone wouldn't or couldn't answer her questions, she'd find someone who could.

She'd headed back out of the cemetery, filled with resolve—until she'd passed the newest grave. It bore only a tiny marker right now, but the stone next to it told her everything she needed to know: Jenny Wallace Gallagher, Beloved Wife and Mother, 1946-1981.

Boone's mother. Buried next to his father, Sam, the man who had brought her here. The man who had hurt his son so much.

She'd been angry with Sam Gallagher for putting Boone and her in an impossible position, but now she wasn't so sure what she felt. The need that swept through her, for family and roots, was not a feeling she welcomed. Longing and discomfort mingled too uncomfortably. She'd let herself need Robert too much when she'd lost her family and almost lost herself in the process. She'd spent her whole life without roots. She shouldn't need any.

Yet as she stared at Jenny Gallagher's headstone,

Maddie wondered if anyone would ever call her "beloved." Being wife and mother had never seemed farther away.

And today's phone call swirled into the mix. It was heady knowledge that a restaurant that her colleagues would kill to work in wanted *her,* Maddie Rose Collins, enough to wait for her to finish out her month. She had options. She could be lionized in the only city that mattered; she could write her own ticket if she did well at Sancerre. And she would do well. She hadn't lied when she told Boone that she was good.

The money she had, combined with what Boone had agreed to pay her for the house, wouldn't be enough to set up her own restaurant in New York, but if she did well at Sancerre, she might attract an investor or two. This time, however, she would hold the majority share. No more penniless Maddie in a one-way partnership like the one she'd had with Robert. And one day, she swore, she would have a place all her own. She'd put down roots, at last.

She had to keep her eye on the prize, to remember her real life and not let the romance of the past sweep her off her feet. She'd learned more than once that romance didn't last, no matter how much she wanted to believe it could.

"Evenin'."

Maddie was so lost in her thoughts that she gasped when Boone spoke up from his seat on the porch.

"I'm sorry. I didn't mean to scare you."

She shook her head. "You didn't, not really. I was just…thinking."

He turned the piece of wood slowly in his hands, studying it with care. Maddie looked more closely and realized that he was whittling it into a shape like—

"Devil! You're carving the puppy's likeness." He was talented, really talented.

Boone shrugged. "Just something to pass the time."

"But it's so lifelike—how long have you been working on it?"

"Just started tonight."

"Boone, you could do these and sell them. That's really good. Have you been doing it a long time?"

"Off and on for years. Sometimes I've had a lot of time I've had to spend waiting."

"Did you take lessons?"

He smiled as though she'd told a joke. "I never heard of whittling lessons. Though I guess I sort of did—my granddaddy used to whittle a lot. He said there was no right way or wrong way. You just start carving and try to miss your own thumb."

She laughed, and when he joined her, something felt a little more right in her world.

"Boone, I'm sorry—"

"Maddie, I'm sorry—"

They both halted abruptly.

"You don't owe me an apology," he said.

"You were right, though, in a way. But I'd rather not make this into an armed camp, Boone. It's only for a few weeks, but I'm not fond of making life harder than it has to be. Maybe you don't need to know my life story, and I know I don't have a right to pry into yours, but I do have some things I really want to know.''

"Like what?'' His eyes were wary.

"I'd like to know about my grandmother. And I'd like to hear about your mother, if you'd tell me about her. If my father loved her, I'd like to know who she was.''

Boone stared at the wood in his hands for so long that she was afraid he didn't intend to answer. Then he looked up at her. ''I was just a little kid when your grandmother died. I don't really remember much about her. I just remember that she seemed very tall, though she was probably only five-eight or so, like you. She was nice to me, but she always seemed sad.''

He shrugged. ''I didn't understand, but I guess we do now, don't we?'' Frown lines appeared between his brows, but he didn't try to deny what Sam's letter had said. ''Sorry. I'm not much help.''

"It's more than I had,'' she whispered.

They were both silent for a long time, listening to the sounds of the night.

Then Boone spoke, but his voice was hushed. ''My mother was probably too soft to be here.''

"On this ranch?''

"On this ranch…with my father…on this earth.'' He drew a deep breath. ''I don't guess she was an angel, but she was as close to one as I'll ever see.''

He looked out across the distance. "She loved to cook, and she liked to laugh. She knew how to make things fun without needing any fancy trimmings. She worked hard, she was always busy. But she was never too busy to read us a story or let us help make cookies."

He glanced up at Maddie. "She was small and pretty, with these big blue eyes and this long blond hair. I used to think when she read me fairy tales that the princesses must have looked like her. No matter that she worked her fingers to the bone—there was always something about her that seemed like she didn't quite belong in this world."

"She must have loved you so much."

He recoiled visibly. "You don't know that."

"No one could feel so loved if it weren't real."

Boone frowned but didn't answer her. Beneath those strong, gentle fingers, a piece of a tree turned into a puppy before her very eyes.

Maddie was so fascinated that she wanted to sit closer and watch him, but the night had been too long, too full of emotions. She yawned before she could stop herself.

"I can't get used to being sleepy so early. In the city, I never get to bed before one or two."

"You're just falling into the natural rhythms of the land."

*But I can't afford to.* She moved toward the door. "I'd better go clean up that kitchen, then head for bed."

"It's already done."

She stopped in her progression across the porch. "You did it?"

One shoulder lifted casually. "You cooked. I cleaned."

"But you put in a very long day already."

"It was my fault you didn't eat. I put your leftovers in the fridge."

Maddie was overwhelmed. Robert had never once lifted a finger. Even her father had treated the kitchen as if it might bite him. The only help she'd ever had was help she paid. "I don't know what to say."

"You don't have to say anything."

"Well, I can say thank you, at least."

"You're welcome. It was a great meal."

Maddie stood at the doorway, one hand gripping the jamb, not sure whether to stay or go. Maybe they *could* be friends, after all. *Go, Maddie, before you screw this up.*

"Well…good night."

"Wait—"

She halted, her hand on the knob.

"I—the private investigator who's looking for Mitch. He needs to go through Sam's things to sift for clues."

Maddie frowned. "And?"

"And it's your house."

"For the moment. He was your father. Those things belonged to him, and now to you."

"I didn't know if you'd mind Marlowe being here."

Maddie turned. "Boone, as far as I'm concerned,

this place is yours, not mine. I'll honor your father's requirement to stay, but I know I'm just a guest. Do whatever you need to do to find your brother.''

She wished that it weren't so dark, so she could see his face more clearly. She felt his stare, but she didn't know what it meant.

Every nerve in her body was already too aware of him. She could still remember all too well how it had felt to have him so close when she'd offered him a taste of the sauce. How much she'd wanted to rise to her toes and place her mouth on his.

The tiny hairs on her body rose in response to him now, and Maddie knew she was in danger of forgetting what was real.

Boone Gallagher was too attractive even when he didn't like her. Tonight, the man who would apologize, the man who cleaned up the kitchen because it was fair—that man was deadly.

''I, uh…I'd better go. Upstairs. To—never mind.'' *Great, Maddie, remind both of you how close you sleep.*

She thought that she could see his eyes glitter in the moonlight.

''Sleep well, Maddie.''

Not likely. ''Good night, Boone.''

She was almost through the door before he spoke again.

''And thank you.''

That voice, so deep…that drawl that slid down her spine and curled low…

Maddie gulped. ''You're welcome.'' As fast as she could go, she was through the door and up the stairs.

## Chapter Six

Boone rolled out of bed and slammed the alarm button down. He wasn't sure why he'd bothered to go to bed. He'd stayed on the porch long after Maddie had left, to be sure they didn't cross paths again upstairs.

But he hadn't been able to stop himself from pausing in front of her closed door. From wanting to open it and watch her sleep in the moonlight. But he wouldn't. Maddie asked too many questions about a past that he wanted to forget. Made him think too much about feelings that did no one any good.

She would open up Pandora's box and then leave for New York, and he would be left here to try to shove everything back inside and slam the box shut.

Heading for the shower this morning, he saw that her door was open, her bed empty. As his path neared the stairwell, he could smell baking bread.

The woman was lethal. She twisted him in knots just with her looks, and then played dirty with her cooking. They weren't playing house, damn it.

He stood with the shower beating down on his head and tried to ignore the traces of Maddie's presence. The perfume of her soap rose in the heated air. A basket of sponges and lotions stood on a stool by the tub. As he scrubbed at a body already worn out by a restless night, a vision of her, naked under this same shower, taunted him.

He turned the shower to Cold.

By the time he got downstairs, he had worked up a fine head of steam, but she wasn't in the kitchen to act as his target.

He realized where she probably was: doing impossible things with that lithe body on the porch.

His porch, damn it.

Boone grabbed a cup of the coffee that had just finished perking. Swearing dark oaths, he burned his tongue by sipping too quickly.

It was suicidal to skip breakfast, considering the physical labor he did in a day. He turned and headed for the barns, anyway.

And there she was, on the porch facing the sunrise, her body stretching as if to greet the sky, her movements slow and graceful.

He hesitated, wanting to watch…just for a minute.

And then she turned.

And smiled. "Good morning."

"Mornin'."

"The bread is almost done."

He had to cut this off now, before it went too far. "I told you not to cook for me."

The peaceful glow dimmed. "I didn't make it for you, but I'm willing to share it."

*Back to kicking puppies, Boone?* "I have to go." He turned to leave.

"With no breakfast?"

"Last I looked, I'd been taking care of myself for a few years."

One glance back at her showed a parade of emotions—hurt, chagrin...the beginnings of anger.

Good. An armed camp was far safer.

"Fine." She squared her shoulders. "If you change your mind, it will be there."

When Maddie turned away, it should have made Boone feel better.

It didn't. As she moved into the next posture, he felt like a kid who'd been sent to the corner, robbed of the fun that the others were having.

But he'd sent *himself* there.

She made him crazy. She made him feel too much. He didn't know how to keep her at a safe distance when she was so damn easygoing. Or how to like himself for trying.

"Thanks for the coffee."

Maddie just nodded and kept going.

Boone headed to the barns, head fuzzy from lack

of sleep and stomach empty of everything but a sour taste, knowing he had no one to blame but himself.

An hour later, Boone saw Maddie walk into the barn with a basket and look around. Jim stepped out of a stall close by and grinned from ear to ear.

"Well, good morning to you, Maddie." Jim sniffed appreciatively.

"Hi, Jim. How are you today?" Maddie returned the smile. She glanced around and spotted Boone. Her smile dimmed.

"I was okay, but by the smell of that basket, I'm hoping I'm about to get a lot better."

"It's cinnamon-oatmeal bread. I don't think Boone had time for breakfast, but even if he did, I thought you and Sonny might enjoy bread fresh from the oven." She shot Boone a sassy glance that dared him to complain.

"Hell—I mean, heck, Maddie, I hope Boone is so stuffed he can't take a bite. It smells great." Without hesitation, he dipped his hand inside. One bite, and he closed his eyes in bliss. "Take me now, Lord. It can't get better than this."

Boone listened to Maddie's laughter and couldn't help smiling himself. His stomach rumbled, and he turned back to the horse he was checking.

"Don't go anywhere, Maddie. I have to feed one more horse. Boone, you stay right where you are until I eat my fill, you hear?"

When Jim walked away, Maddie looked down the barn, straight at Boone. "It's foolish for you to turn this down. You work too hard every day to miss breakfast, just because you're afraid of me.''

The woman definitely had a mouth on her.

Boone stepped out of the stall, latching the door, and snorted. ''The day I'm afraid of you is the day the sun comes up in the west.''

Maddie smiled like the Sphinx. ''Then you'll have some, I take it.''

His stomach was yelling at him to dive into that basket, but he held back.

''I know this is awkward, Boone. The whole situation is not what either of us wants, but we just have to make the best of it. You don't have to like me for us to get along.''

Beside her now, Boone's hand stopped in midair. ''I never said I disliked you.'' Hell, he liked too much about her.

The quick flare of something dark and almost hurt in her eyes surprised him.

But before he could figure out what to say next, she opened the cloth covering the basket and held the basket closer to him, changing the subject. ''So these are your horses?''

Boone's mouth was too full of heaven for him to do more than nod.

She glanced at Slow Dance, the palomino stallion on which he was hoping to build his future. ''Who is that? He's really handsome, isn't he?''

Boone swallowed. ''You ride?''

Maddie smiled, almost bashfully. ''No, but I've always thought it would be wonderful.''

"You don't want to try one like Slow Dance for your first horse. He's pretty even-tempered for a stallion, but that's not saying much."

"You'd let me ride one?" Her eyes were wide as saucers.

Oh, hell. What had he just done? When what he most needed was to stay as far away from her as possible, here he'd gone and opened the door to their spending more time together.

But he couldn't take it back now, not when she looked like that. You'd think he'd handed her diamonds from Tiffany's.

He could make it Jim's job, and he probably should. But something within him balked at the thought of not being the first one to see Maddie's delight, if it meant that much to her.

"It's okay, Boone. I understand. You're too busy."

Boone focused on her and saw the disappointment cloud her expression. A man who would dim Maddie's glow ought to be shot.

"I can make some time, if you can be flexible."

Maddie lit up like the sun at noonday. "You just tell me when."

Her gaze on him was so warm and soft that Boone's own gaze lingered, while a thousand thoughts danced in his head. Her lips were slightly parted, her breasts rising and falling in the rhythm of her excitement. Boone wanted more than he'd ever wanted anything in his life to take her to the ground, right then and there. To seek within Maddie the warmth that his cold, dark soul craved.

"Hoo-ey, Maddie girl, I'm dying for another taste of that—" Jim stopped in his tracks.

Maddie stepped back from Boone, her cheeks flaming.

Boone turned away, not sure whether to thank Jim—or strangle him.

Maddie rose to the occasion. "Boone's going to teach me to ride, Jim. Isn't that exciting?"

Boone caught Jim's startled glance out of the corner of his eye. When Jim's weathered face began to crease into a knowing grin, Boone shot him a glare that should have fried him where he stood.

But Jim just grinned more broadly.

"Well now, that's real fine, Maddie. There's no one better to teach you than Boone here. He's the finest horseman any of us ever saw."

Boone felt Maddie's gaze studying him, and was surprised when his own cheeks warmed.

"I saw how gentle his hands were on that colt. I was impressed, Boone. I thought cowboys broke horses with spurs and that sort of thing."

Boone turned. "That's the old way, and some people still use it. I prefer to let a horse believe that it's his idea to work with me. There's no need to break his spirit. You start him early before he knows his own strength, and you teach him to trust you. He needs to respect you and know you mean business, but it's not your business to be mean."

Boone stopped, feeling as if he was talking too much.

But Maddie's eyes gleamed with curiosity...and warmth. "That's beautiful. It was wonderful to watch you with him."

Boone felt for a moment as if he stood on the edge of a magic circle—a private space he could share with Maddie if he'd take another step or two. But he sensed Jim watching them both avidly, while snatching another slice of bread.

Whether or not he could keep himself away from her as he knew he surely should, Boone wasn't conducting the dance with Maddie in public.

So he pushed her away with words. "I've got to get back to work."

He saw her hunch her shoulders slightly as if absorbing a blow, but very quickly she squared her posture and shook that mane of hair. "Of course. I need to get on to the garden, anyway. I'll just leave the bread right here." She turned away and set the basket on a shelf nailed to the wall.

Jim shot him a glare. Boone refused to respond. It was what had to happen, damn it. He couldn't let go with her.

He would do his best to get along, and he would teach her to ride the way he'd teach any other student. But he would use the control that had kept his head on straight in the midst of danger; he would use the discipline that had marked his life for years; and he would keep his hands off Maddie Rose Collins.

If it killed him.

But as he watched her walk away toward the garden, he couldn't quite hold the line. "Maddie," he called out.

The dark hair swung, glistening in the morning light as she turned.

"Maybe tomorrow we can start your lessons."

Her smile was quick, her nod enthusiastic, before she turned back and walked away.

Maddie forgave too easily. And it seemed that he was always handing her something that needed forgiveness.

"Maddie," Jim called out.

She turned back once more. "Have all you want, Jim."

"Oh, I intend to, but that's not what I wanted. Are you going to let Boone here take you to the rodeo dance tonight?"

Her whole face lit up. "A rodeo dance?"

He would kill Jim, Boone thought, the minute Maddie was out of sight.

"Yep. Ever been to one?" asked Jim.

She shook her head. "No, but I love to dance." Then she went very still. "But Boone doesn't have to take me. Just tell me where to find it."

Boone bit down on a groan. "I guess I can take you."

Maddie's shoulders went stiff. "I'm a big girl. I can go by myself. I've lived in New York. Morning Star can't be too tough." She looked away from Boone. "Can you give me the directions, Jim?"

Jim muttered under his breath. "Sure, I can. But I'll do you one better—Velda and I will pick you up and take you."

Maddie's smile was tentative. "Would Velda mind?"

"Aw, hell—I mean, heck, no. Velda would love havin' a woman to chatter to."

Her smile reached full wattage. "Then, thank you. I'd love to go."

"We'll pick you up at seven. You like barbecue?"

"You bet." Maddie hesitated. "Well, I guess I'd better get to work in the garden. Thank you, Jim." She pointedly ignored Boone.

"Thank you for the bread. We'll see you this evenin'."

When Maddie was out of sight, Jim turned on him. "You're a damn fool, Boone Gallagher."

Boone shot him a quick glance, then headed to saddle up Slow Dance. "I didn't ask you."

"You hurt that little gal's feelings. What would it hurt you to take her to the dance?"

"I don't want to talk about it."

"She could be the best thing that ever happened to you."

"She won't stay."

"How do you know?"

"I know."

"Because she's from the city, like Helen? You didn't cause Helen's problems."

"She'd be alive if not for me." *And so would my baby.*

"Maddie isn't Helen."

Boone rounded on him. "She's on a vacation, Jim. Anything can be fun for a little while. She's got places in New York begging for her to come back up there. Why would she want to be stuck on a ranch in Morning Star?"

"Nobody said you had to marry her. Just enjoy her while she's here."

Boone's temper spiked. "Don't you go talking like Maddie is only good for a quick roll in the hay. She deserves better than that."

Then Jim smiled and shook his head. "I never said she didn't. So give her better."

"I'm not condemning another woman to a life she would hate."

"Damn, but I'm going to be glad when she leaves, even though I'll miss her. You're like a lion with a thorn in his paw, and it ain't gonna get any better until you do something about it."

"There's nothing to do, Jim, except wait. She'll be gone soon enough. And so will you, if you don't get back to work."

Jim snorted. "Like you think you could run this place without me." His grin didn't fade.

"Go away and leave me alone. I've got work to do."

Jim started to turn, then hesitated. "If you got any sense in that head of yours, you'll be at that dance tonight. I can't keep watch over Maddie and Velda both, and you and I both know Maddie's going to be a powerful temptation to those cowboys.''

Boone curled his lip. ''It's not my business. She said it herself—she's a big girl.''

Jim watched him for a minute, then he started chuckling. ''You know, this is gonna be fun to watch, is all I got to say. That is, if we don't kill you first.''

Boone shot him a glare. ''I only wish I could believe that was all you had to say. The day you quit jawin' at me is the day we put you in the ground. Now go away.''

Jim tipped his hat and walked away, whistling.

Maddie paused while pulling weeds in the garden when she saw Boone and Slow Dance leave the barn. When they moved into a gallop across the pasture, it was a sight that she knew she'd never forget.

Golden man and golden horse. The two moved together as if formed from one flesh. It was a ballet of rugged strength, smooth and sinuous, Boone's strong thighs and the horse's muscled flanks making the breath catch in her throat. She felt as though she'd stepped back in time, as though Boone and the horse and the land were part of one another. The sight stirred her at a primal level, and she watched them until she could see them no more.

Then she rolled off her heels and sat back on the ground, smelling the tang of the tomato vines where she'd brushed them, reaching for weeds.

Around her she heard the soft call of cattle, the

occasional nicker of a horse in the barn. Birds in the live oak trees around the house sang "hello" to the morning.

But even with all that, it was so quiet compared to what she'd known. Maddie felt the warm earth beneath her, the wind ruffling her hair, and she knew a moment of contentment so peaceful and deep that it almost seemed holy.

She closed her eyes and let the sun warm her face, the breeze kiss her lips, and in that moment, Maddie thought she knew why her father had never told her about this place. It must have torn a hole in his heart the size of Texas to grow up belonging to this place—and then to become a pariah.

All the anger and confusion Maddie had felt toward her father evaporated like the morning's dew in the face of the sun. She understood now why he'd done it. To speak of this place and know he could never return would have been torture.

*I understand, Daddy. And I'm so very sorry.*

He must have felt like Adam cast out from Paradise. Just watching Boone and knowing how this place formed so much of who he was, seeing the pain that lingered from the years he'd been forced away, gave Maddie a sense of what leaving must have cost her father.

That he had done it to save his mother, that he had known everyone else important to him would think him a murderer, seemed to Maddie to be a deed as noble as anything she'd ever heard or read.

That Sam had denied him the chance to return was a tragedy, a betrayal of staggering proportions.

For the first time, Maddie truly understood why Sam had given her this place. He had to know what it would have cost Dalton to lose it. Sam also knew how it felt to lose Jenny. And by his actions, he had condemned her father to needless years as an outcast from both the place and the woman he loved.

But if Sam had looked for her father, what would have happened? She was a child then. If her father had come back here, what would her life have been like? What would have happened to her, to Boone and Mitch, if Dalton and Jenny had wanted to be together?

It was all too confusing—and all water under the bridge. And much as this place now pulled at Maddie, there remained the fact that she couldn't make a living here. She had a life and a career back east; here she had nothing but other people's broken dreams.

Drawing in a deep breath, Maddie sent a promise heavenward to her father. *I understand, Daddy, and I will soak in all of this that I can before I must leave. Someday I will tell your story to a new generation. I won't let your heritage die. I just hope you understand all the reasons why I can't possibly stay.*

Then with a heavy sigh, Maddie bent back to her weeding.

Boone drove up to the community center that night, asking himself for the fifteenth time why he wasn't at home enjoying the silence.

Maddie would be fine. She was a big girl. Jim was there.

He would just watch for a while, then he would leave.

After parking his truck, Boone stepped out and heard the music blaring. How long had it been since he'd attended a dance? Helen had turned her nose up at country music—would Maddie be doing the same?

Would she mentally be poking fun at the rubes? Would the music grate on her nerves? A part of Boone readied himself to defend the people and the place he loved from mockery. These were good people. They worked hard and had little to show for their efforts, either in material goods or life-style options.

Simple people were the salt of the earth. He had missed them all.

Boone nodded to various old acquaintances, noting the tipped hats and smiles. He stopped to visit with neighboring ranchers, and quickly discovered that word had spread of the interloper city-slicker who had come to town.

Boone was surprised to find himself defending Maddie, more surprised to find himself scanning the crowd inside for her presence.

It didn't take long.

She was a flame, glowing in the darkness. Around

her circled the moths, batting their wings and court-
ing annihilation.

Boone watched her. And he burned.

Standing against a support post in the darkness,
he saw the fire and the fun that was Maddie. In full
gypsy regalia, Maddie reigned as belle of the ball.
Her red halter top glowed against pale satin skin, the
full froth of her short red-and-gold skirt showing off
the legs that haunted his dreams.

But it was Maddie's spirit that glowed the bright-
est as she danced and laughed. She didn't know the
steps—that much was obvious—but her good nature
and natural grace made that unimportant. Surrounded by partners more than willing to teach her,
Maddie learned quickly. He watched her do the Cot-
ton-Eyed Joe and the schottische, her legs flashing
and drawing every male eye in the place. When she
missed a step, her laughter brought smiles to every
face.

Maddie's easy affection charmed them all. Sour
old women found no fault, for Maddie was unfail-
ingly polite and never favored anyone. She could not
be branded "easy," but her sensuality wove a spell
around every man in the hall. Yet the women smiled
at her obvious sense of fun, at her willingness to
poke fun at herself.

The City Girl had made herself at home.

Boone watched his neighbors with amazement,
these people who were never rude but didn't take
kindly to strangers. One by one, they accepted Maddie into the fold.

It was torture to watch her, to see her move into the arms of old men and boys: young studs eager to show off, and older men who wanted to claim her.

He wanted to step out of the darkness and tell every one of them to get lost.

But Maddie wasn't his. She was only visiting.

Boone felt a gaze on him and turned to the left. Jim nodded toward Maddie and lifted his beer in a salute. His taunting challenge hung in the air.

First thing tomorrow, Boone was sending Jim to walk the fence line. Not ride. *Walk.*

He merely lifted a negligent eyebrow and turned away from his foreman.

He felt it the moment Maddie saw him.

Her gaze halted on his before moving back to the cowboy whose hand rested on her hip. Boone ground his teeth and meant to look away.

But he couldn't.

Instead, he glared at the man who had the nerve to touch her, even while he recognized that Maddie was a free agent.

He had no claim on her. He never would.

Tearing his gaze away, Boone turned to the first person he saw, Etta Mae Rodgers. Sixty-five if she was a day, Etta Mae had never married but had educated many a child in this town, including Boone.

"How are you, Ms. Rodgers?"

"Boone Gallagher, as I live and breathe. It's good to have you back."

Her eagerness warmed him. "Thank you. It's good to be here."

"I'm sorry about your father."

Boone tensed, then muttered the expected. "He'd been sick for a while."

"No, Boone, I mean I'm sorry about this mess he's left you. Sam Gallagher used to be a lovely young man, one of this town's real gifts—but he changed after your mother died. He was wrong in what he did to you and Mitch."

Boone's surprise must have shown, for she carried on. "You thought no one noticed? People noticed, all right, but it isn't our way to interfere. Maybe we should have done something. We don't have so much that we can afford to lose good men like yourself and your brother."

Boone was sure his mouth must be hanging open. He cleared his throat. "Well…thank you."

She waved it away. "No need to thank me. I'm as guilty as any for standing aside. But I don't intend to stand aside now. If you need any help getting rid of that Yankee, you just let me know."

Just then, Boone felt a hand on his arm and turned. "That Yankee" stood beside him, her smile fading.

"Uh…Ms. Rodgers, this is Maddie Rose Collins."

"You're Dalton Wheeler's daughter, is that right?"

Maddie gripped Boone's arm tightly, but drew herself up very straight. "Yes. I am." Her tone dared the woman to say anything derogatory.

"Humph," Etta Mae muttered. "Sam created a mess for Boone."

Boone saw Maddie swallow and struggle for composure. When she spoke, her tone held a bite. "My father didn't kill anyone, Mrs.—?"

"Rodgers. *Ms.* Rodgers." Etta Mae's tone broadcast her doubts. "Everyone has known for years that—"

"My father did a noble deed," Maddie interrupted, her silver eyes flashing fire. "He took the blame for something he didn't do so that his mother wouldn't go to jail for defending herself."

"The Caswells are a respected family around here."

Maddie's jaw jutted. "I can't respect a man who beats on women."

Etta Mae's nostrils flared. Her color rose. She opened her mouth to retort, but Boone stepped in.

"It's true, Ms. Rodgers. Dalton didn't hurt anyone. Folks were wrong in what they thought. He took the blame and exiled himself to keep his mother safe."

Boone saw Maddie's startled glance, the look of gratitude in her gaze. He turned back to see Etta Mae's frown.

"Surely you can't condone what your father did— giving your house to a—"

In another situation, Boone would have laughed at how Maddie puffed up like a mama hen, prepared to defend Sam. Instead, he stepped in to defuse the situation.

"Ms. Rodgers, I can't control what my father did or didn't do. All I can do is deal with it. Ms. Collins is caught in a bad situation and is doing her best. Now if you'll excuse us, I believe Ms. Collins has promised me this dance." Then he turned and led Maddie away.

She was fuming. "That old biddy. Is that how they all feel? Like I'm an interloper? The daughter of a murderer who's come to feed off the remains like a vulture?"

He pulled her into a dark corner, then grabbed her shoulders and turned her to face him.

Tears welled in her eyes, and he couldn't stand it.

"She doesn't matter, Maddie. People talk. Around here, they don't have much else to do."

"It *does* matter. I can't stand that they're thinking about my father like that. He did nothing wrong. He gave up everything that mattered to him. I don't know why he would love this place, when people are so ready to believe the worst of him. It's not right. I have to defend—" She turned away, ready to head back toward Etta Mae.

He gripped her tightly and pulled her against him, cupping her cheek with one hand. "Listen to me."

Maddie's face held mutiny, but slowly she lifted her gaze. The hurt he saw there touched him.

"We know the truth, you and I. What does it matter to you, when you'll be leaving? They're just a bunch of country people who will never set foot in one of your restaurants. Why do you care?"

Tears leaked from the corners of her eyes. "I care.

For the sake of my father and grandmother, I care. They would have cared. These were their neighbors. They would have been mine, too, if—''

Boone stroked her jaw. ''No, they wouldn't have. If Dalton had stayed, you wouldn't have been born.''

Maddie glanced away, her head shaking slowly from side to side. ''I don't belong here,'' she whispered.

He knew that, only too well. But he had to do something to ease her pain. ''I'll make them understand, Maddie. I'll make sure they know what your father gave up.''

She turned a look on him so luminous and grateful that Boone stood, transfixed. For a long moment, she studied him as if trying to understand him.

''Why would you do that?''

''It's only fair.''

''I've caused you a lot of problems. I know you'll be glad for me to leave.''

Tempting words stuck in his throat. *You don't have to leave. You could stay.* If only he didn't know better, know what it would cost her in the long run.

''You didn't make this situation. Neither of us did.''

She smiled sadly. ''A few more weeks, and it's over.'' She sounded relieved.

Boone dropped his hand and stepped back. ''Yeah. Not that long.'' Not long, hell—*eternity.* When viewed through the glass of time spent trying to resist Maddie, the days stretched out forever.

Twenty-five days of too much…and not enough.

She turned away and watched the dance floor, where the band was tuning up again. She drew in a deep breath, then shuddered, seeming to arm herself.

Then she spoke, her voice wistful. "Did you mean that about the next dance?"

The last thing he needed was to hold Maddie in his arms, but he'd just have to hope the next dance was a fast one. He couldn't refuse her. "Sure."

Her smile blinded him. "You like to dance?"

Boone shrugged. "I get along."

Some of Maddie's sparkle flared. She grabbed his hand and pulled. "Well, come on, cowboy. Let's dance."

Despite his better sense, Boone gripped her hand and headed for the dance floor. When the band struck up a quick two-step, he wasn't as happy as he should have been. But it didn't take long to start enjoying himself. Maddie was a graceful dancer and quickly fell in step with him. Soon they moved together as if from long experience.

"You ever done this before?" he asked.

Maddie shook her head, eyes shining. "No, but I love it."

"Hick music not too boring for you?"

She batted his shoulder. "Don't be a snob, Boone."

"Me?"

"Yes, you. I know Helen was from the city, and I'm sorry she didn't like it, but you're being worse than a snob—you're a bigot."

"Bigot?"

"Yeah, bigot." Her eyes challenged him. "You think the only people who can appreciate this place are those who were born here?"

Boone stopped where they stood, not caring that other dancers bumped into them, complaining. "Don't try to tell me you like this place."

"I do like it."

"But you won't stay."

Maddie met his gaze. "I don't have to stay to like it. I'd—I'd like to come back and visit sometime." Her gaze turned hesitant. "Would that bother you?"

Hell, yes, it would bother him. Saying goodbye to her and knowing she might pop back in, anytime she pleased? That he'd get used to having her around, then she'd disappear whenever the mood took her?

She saw his reaction. Her face reflected her disappointment. "That's okay," she said casually. "It was just an idea. I probably won't get much time, anyway. I usually try to make it to Europe once a year to keep up on developments there."

Dancers around them were complaining loudly. Boone shot glares all around, but began to move across the floor once again. He didn't look at Maddie as he answered. "I hadn't thought about it. It might be all right."

Maddie shook her head, then studied their feet. "Please—don't be so enthusiastic."

"Hey, I never thought about it, all right? I don't know how I feel."

She glanced up. "Do you ever let yourself really

feel, Boone?'' she asked, her eyes soft and searching.

The music slowed and segued into a waltz. Boone found himself reluctant to take her off the floor and let her go. Instead, he moved into the new steps, and Maddie moved effortlessly with him.

"I don't know what you want me to say, Maddie."

Maddie looked at him with sad eyes. He felt as though he'd disappointed her. "I want you to say what's in your heart. To let go and just feel."

She didn't, though. Not really, he thought. If he once let go of his control, she wouldn't like what she saw. Boone didn't much like it himself. He was a man who had loved one woman badly, who had never earned his father's love. He'd lost a child who should have had a chance if he'd just done things right.

He'd been good in the dark arts of killing and war. He could track an enemy to extinction, could find a grain of sand in the desert. None of those were skills Maddie would admire.

She was a creature of light, and he was darkness. She might think she wanted to know him, but she was wrong.

Since Boone had no answers Maddie would want to hear, he didn't even try. Instead, he pulled her close and let the music fill the silence.

She held stiff for a moment, but he didn't relent. Soon she softened and swayed against him, and Boone knew a moment of painful longing.

Maddie had weapons of her own.

A soft, tender heart.

A ready smile.

A soul that shone more brightly than the sun.

Maddie took the whole world to her bosom and cherished it. A part of Boone wanted to step into the magic circle and inhale Maddie's cheer, her never-say-die optimism—to hold it as a talisman against the darkness inside him.

But Boone knew his own power. His darkness would snuff out her light and the world would be poorer.

So Boone just held Maddie close until the music faded.

And then he thanked her, turned her over to the line of men waiting for the belle of the ball—and walked away without looking back.

Maddie watched him walk away, so tall and handsome in the starched white shirt, knife-edged crease in his jeans. She wondered when she'd ever learn to keep her thoughts to herself. Hadn't she warned herself that it wouldn't work for her to come back to visit? He hadn't answered her, which was answer enough in itself.

When she left Morning Star, she would not return.

"You ready to dance, pretty girl?" The cowboy asking the question smiled beneath his straw hat and stepped forward.

*An adventure, Maddie. Remember, it's just an ad-*

*venture. You were having fun until Boone showed up.*

She accepted the outstretched hand and smiled her biggest smile. Not from the heart, but it had always been Maddie's belief that if you smiled whether you felt like it or not, you'd soon feel better. "Let's do it, Mr.—?"

"Call me Randy, ma'am."

"Then you call me Maddie."

"Here we go, Maddie. I like it fast."

"Good." She would concentrate on her feet and forget the heart Boone had bruised.

Twenty-five days and counting. The end couldn't come too soon.

Boone stayed outside for a long time, staring into the moonlight. He was lousy company; soon, even Jim left him alone. He nursed the same beer he'd been holding since he'd walked off the dance floor, less interested in something to drink than having something to do with his hands.

He could still feel her soft curves against him, feel her warm breath on his chest where his shirt parted. He could smell Maddie's scent, unnameable and mysterious, rich and full of sex and sunshine and…sin.

Why couldn't he just take what she would give and enjoy it while she stayed? What was it about Maddie that made this so damn hard?

So what if she was leaving? He'd had affairs before, had left and been left, had enjoyed rolling on the bed and parting unencumbered. Why not with Maddie?

*Because she's not a roll in the hay.* Just that simple.

Maddie was more. If he played with fire, he would be burned, but playing with Maddie could incinerate him. He knew it in his bones.

A shiver ran down his spine. Boone grimaced in disgust. Maddie's fanciful thinking was rubbing off on him.

Shoving off from the pillar on which he leaned, Boone drained his beer bottle on the grass and took it back inside to the bar. He planned to tell Jim he was leaving and make sure Maddie had a ride home.

Until he took one quick glance at the dance floor and didn't like what he saw.

Hank Ransom was Maddie's partner, and Maddie didn't look happy at all.

Boone and Hank went way back. Hank had a vicious streak. In school, Boone had been the only one around who would go toe-to-toe with him. Hank's crooked nose had come courtesy of Boone, and Hank had never forgotten it.

Boone cared nothing about their past. All he cared about was that Hank was holding Maddie way too close. He started through the crowd, watching carefully to be sure that he wasn't mistaken. When Maddie pushed at Hank's chest and tried to back away, Hank jerked her back.

Boone saw red. He picked up speed, shoving through the crowd. But when he got close to them, he slowed down, remembering what he'd once seen Hank do to a reluctant girlfriend. He had to handle this carefully, or Maddie could get hurt.

"Evenin', Hank," Boone drawled.

Hank kept a tight grip on Maddie and turned, nodding. "Hey, Boone. Heard you were back."

Boone shot Maddie a worried glance, then choked back a grin. If Hank gave her an inch to maneuver, he was going to find himself unmanned. Maddie wasn't scared yet—she looked mad as the devil.

But Boone knew Hank was truly dangerous. "Let's go outside and catch up on old times, Hank."

Maddie glared at him. Impatience vibrated from her every pore. "Let go of me, you big, fat—oaf—"

Boone grabbed Maddie's arm and turned suddenly, wedging his shoulder in between them. With practiced ease, he slid Maddie away and behind him. "I don't think the lady is enjoying herself."

Hank's little pig eyes narrowed. "She was dancing with me. We weren't finished."

"Well, you see, Hank, there's just one problem. I was never very good at sharing."

"She's not yours. You weren't here. You left."

"But I was coming back. And here I am." Boone kept his voice smooth. He didn't see how Hank could miss the implied threat. He wouldn't welcome the fight, but Hank couldn't have forgotten who had usually wound up on top.

He pulled Maddie close. "You go on and find yourself another girl, Hank. This one's taken." Turning away, he walked Maddie toward the exit.

They had almost reached the door when Maddie was wrenched from his arms. Hank jerked her to him and grabbed her hair, grinding his mouth down on hers.

Boone went blind with rage. He leapt toward them. Grabbing Hank by the arm, he jerked him away from Maddie. The solid connection of fist to jaw didn't begin to placate the roar in his head.

Hank had put his mouth on Maddie. Had hurt Maddie.

Boone never heard the shouting around him. He entered a zone of deadly silence, a savage place where forsaken skills had lain dormant. With brutal satisfaction, he punished Hank for daring to hurt Maddie's bright spirit, for endangering the light she had brought into his life.

"Boone, stop—please—" Finally, Maddie's voice sliced through the rage.

He looked at her, her face drained of all color. Then he looked back at Hank, collapsed against the wall, chest heaving.

"You crazy sonofa—" Hank roared. "She's the spawn of a murderer—you're welcome to her," he spat.

Boone charged toward him, but Maddie held on for dear life to one arm, while Jim grabbed him by the other, stepping between him and Hank.

"Come on now, Boone. Back away. He's crazy and mean. You know that. Come on. You're scaring Maddie."

The last words broke through to him. Boone

looked down at her and saw her eyes had gone huge and dark.

Now he'd done it. She'd seen what lay inside him: the dark, howling beast that had saved his life in the past was now his damnation.

He turned to Hank. ''You're not fit to walk on the same ground as Maddie. If I ever hear you talking about her like that again, I'll—''

''Boone, please.'' Maddie's quiet voice settled him as nothing else could.

But he wasn't quite through. ''You stay away from her, you hear me? You stay very far away.''

Hank didn't respond. He turned and lumbered off, leaning on a friend.

Then Boone realized that his eye hurt like hell. He reached up, and his hand came away with blood on it.

''I'll drive you home in your truck,'' Jim offered. ''Maddie can come later with Velda.''

Boone looked at Maddie, prepared for her revulsion. Instead he saw quiet strength.

''That's all right, Jim,'' she said. ''If Boone can't see to drive, I can drive his truck. We'll be all right.''

Jim looked back and forth between them. ''You sure about that, Maddie?''

His meaning was clear. Boone wasn't fit to be with her.

She nodded and clutched Boone's arm tightly. ''Yes. I'm sure.'' Then she looked up at Boone. ''Can you drive, or would you like me to do it?''

He felt unclean, contaminated by the anger that had spewed from him. "I can get myself home. No need for you to come."

She reached for a bar towel someone had brought over. Lifting it to his face with careful strokes, she mopped away the blood. Then she looked him straight in the eye. "Don't trip over that pride, Boone. You took care of me. Now let me take care of you."

Her calm voice and matter-of-fact manner stirred his hope. Could it be that she wasn't frightened by what she'd seen? Boone studied her as carefully as she was watching him. Then he shook his head. "You always surprise me."

The smile that was never far away reappeared. "Good. Don't forget you said that." Then she clasped his hand. "Take me home, Boone."

For one quicksilver, impossible moment, Boone let himself imagine a life where those words could be ordinary.

*Take me home, Boone.*

They weren't real. He knew that.

But for tonight, at least, he was the man who had the right to take Maddie home.

He squeezed her hand and led her outside.

## Chapter Seven

Stubborn. A frying pan applied to the side of Boone's head looked more attractive all the time. He'd insisted on driving, denying that he was hurt. Maddie tamped down her concerns, her thoughts still on what had happened.

Some women would have called it Neanderthal— Boone's reaction back there. Maddie tried to imagine a single man she'd ever known who would leap to her defense with such raw physical power.

None came to mind. She tried to picture Robert in that same situation. Robert would have used words or bouncers—or walked away.

Boone had defended her honor with his fists.

As a thinking woman of the nineties, she should have been horrified. Such brute behavior should have revolted her.

It hadn't. She wasn't.

Instead, Maddie was thrilled. She felt safe. Protected. Awed by what Boone had done.

Boone would have mashed in Robert's face for what he'd done to her. Boone would have dispatched the bullies who had taunted the gangly girl, Maddie, who had never fit in.

She'd been angry at first, but Hank's strength had frightened her when he squeezed her more tightly, spewing sour beer breath in her face. When he'd ground his mouth down on hers, she'd been more frightened than on any dark New York street.

Then, like an avenging angel, Boone had charged to her rescue, his golden hair gleaming in the light—

The hair rose on her skin as she remembered him, the sheer power and strength of his passion to protect her.

She'd thought that she'd never see Boone lose his formidable control. Now she knew why he clamped down so hard.

It wasn't because he didn't feel. Far from it.

Boone felt too much.

If only that passion could be spent on her.... What must it be like? Maddie rubbed her arms at the thought and squirmed on the seat.

"You cold?" He reached out to turn down the air-conditioning.

Maddie looked over at him, but he turned away quickly. Since they'd left, silence had wrapped him like a shroud. He wouldn't meet her gaze.

"Boone, I didn't thank you for what you did back there."

"You mean for acting like some kind of beast let out of his cage?"

She jerked around to see if he was joking. His face was grim.

"You weren't an animal. You rescued me."

Boone pulled up to the house and turned off the truck. Still not meeting her gaze, he stared straight ahead. "I'm sorry you saw that."

"Boone..." She reached out and laid one hand on his arm.

He pulled away and opened his door. In the overhead light, she saw anguish on his face.

Boone left the truck and headed for the house, not waiting for her.

Maddie leapt out of her side and followed, racing to catch up. Just before the porch steps, she grabbed his arm.

He spun around. "Don't—" he barked. "Let me be."

"Boone, what's wrong?"

"Go away, Maddie." When she showed no intention of leaving, he turned away toward the barn.

Something deep within her said not to let him leave like this. She practically ran to get in front of him.

"Maddie..." His voice dropped to a growl.

She got a better look at him in the moonlight. His face was all angles and haunted hollows. "Talk to me, Boone. Tell me what's wrong."

He rounded on her then. "I could have killed him. I would have, if you and Jim——" He looked away, his jaw working. "You shouldn't have seen that."

"You saved me, Boone. He was hurting me. I was scared."

Boone exhaled a shuddering breath. He looked away.

Maddie reached up and laid her hands on either side of his face. "Boone…let me in. Please."

The face he turned to her could have been terrifying. To Maddie, it screamed of inner pain, of a man balanced on a razor's edge.

All Maddie could do was hold very still. And hold on to him.

Suddenly, he reached for her like a drowning man clawing for shore. With a strength that should have frightened her, Boone pulled her into his body.

But Maddie wasn't afraid. Deep within her, she knew this man would never hurt her. He would hurt himself instead.

Then the time for thought was over. Boone lowered his head to hers and took her mouth.

All around her, Maddie felt his strength, his power. She yielded to Boone, welcoming him inside her mouth, parched almost to dying for his kiss.

Boone couldn't think at all. The events of the night, the shuddery debris of adrenaline rage, the too-long pent-up need—all ganged up on him and sent his control careening toward the brink.

He wanted her. It was all he knew. Maddie—the taste of her, the scent of her in his nostrils, the feel of her under his hands... Boone's ears roared with the wanting, deaf to all sense, to all logic.

Boone breathed Maddie into his lungs, absorbed her through his skin. Like a creature of night thrust into sunlight, he was assaulted by too many feelings, too much need. He slid trembling fingers beneath her skirt and sought her warmth, shuddering with the power of his craving.

Maddie arched her back and pressed her mound against him, fingertips gliding through his hair until her nails scraped his scalp.

Boone didn't care. She could claw her way down his body and he would welcome the pain. All he knew was that he had to be inside her, had to bury himself deep. He gripped her tighter.

Until Maddie tensed and whimpered.

Then, like cold water drenching his ardor, reality slapped Boone back into the moment. Into the harsh, cold world of what could not be.

He jerked away, staring at her. What the hell was he doing? How was he any different from Hank? He had to get away from her before he ruined everything.

Without a word, he headed for the barn.

Maddie watched him go, torn and confused. She'd been ready for him, swept away by his passion. The power of her own response still shocked her.

Like the man of stone, Boone walked away. This time, she didn't try to stop him, for deep within her stirred a knowledge of the true danger.

He *could* hurt her. Not her body—she didn't fear that. Something much worse.

If she let him do this, make love to her as both of them craved, there would be no turning back.

She had to remember that no matter how much she'd enjoyed this respite, this wasn't where she belonged. She had new friends to make, a career to build. She would someday own a place of her own.

There was nothing for her here but a man who didn't want to want her—and the echoes of a troubled past.

Even if they could overcome all that, what would she do here? It wasn't an option to ask Boone to leave here and go with her. He belonged in this place as much as anyone she'd ever known.

She could make love with Boone on this night, but if she did, she already knew what would happen. Boone would show her passion like nothing she'd ever experienced.

But it wouldn't change reality.

She couldn't stay, and Boone wouldn't leave.

Better to stop now before he broke her heart.

The next afternoon, Maddie headed for the barn. Boone had risen even earlier than usual, surprising her by leaving a note saying that he would be gone all day, but that he'd try to get back by four o'clock for her first riding lesson.

She'd spent the day cleaning a house that Vondell had left perfectly clean. Maddie wasn't much of a housekeeper, but she needed to stay busy.

She tried to work up the same excitement she'd felt yesterday about learning to ride—before Boone had kissed her. She did want to learn, but she didn't want to face Boone.

*Nonsense. You're made of sterner stuff, Maddie.*

Squaring her shoulders, she headed toward the pen behind the barn.

And there he was, intent on saddling a horse smaller than either horse she'd seen Boone ride.

The mare moved away as Maddie approached, and Boone reached out to stroke her neck. "Easy, Fancy." Without turning, he spoke to Maddie. "Come on over to my left side, near her head where she can see you clearly."

Maddie didn't know how he'd known it was her, but she didn't worry about it. She was far more concerned about the horse. It was one thing to think about riding, another to be next to one. Gingerly, she approached.

Boone finished fastening something on the saddle and patted the horse's rump. "It's okay, Fancy. Maddie's a friend."

The tone soothed, just as it had soothed the colt the other day. Maddie marveled that he could be so calm. It was as if last night had never happened.

Until he looked at her. For just one second, Maddie thought Boone might not be as calm as he seemed.

His voice gave nothing away, however. "Reach out your hand, palm upward, and let her smell you.

Like this.'' He demonstrated, strong fingers out-stretched, wide palm open.

The mare snuffled at his palm, then shook her head.

Maddie couldn't help jumping.

''She won't hurt you. She's very gentle, and quite the lady, aren't you, Fancy girl?'' Boone's voice wooed her.

''That's her name? Fancy?''

''Fancy Free.''

Maddie smiled and cast him a quick glance. ''I like it. My kind of name.''

A quick grin skipped across Boone's face.

Maddie drew a deep breath and stretched her hand open, holding it beneath the horse's muzzle.

The mare blew puffs of air across her palm. Little hairs brushed her skin. Maddie giggled. ''It tickles.''

A quick glance showed Boone grinning. ''Yeah. Give me your hand.''

Maddie moved it away, holding it out to Boone.

He dropped a sugar cube in her palm. ''Now hold it out again. She'll be your friend for life. Fancy's got a real sweet tooth.''

Love of the horse suffused his voice.

Maddie put her palm back in front of Fancy's muzzle. When the mare lipped at her palm, it was all Maddie could do to keep still.

Boone chuckled. ''I've done it for so many years, I don't notice the sensation.''

Now Fancy's head swung toward Maddie, butting her arm.

Maddie wouldn't let herself step away, reaching out on instinct to pet the front of her head, just below the eyes.

"That's right. Stroke her there and talk to her. Stroke her neck, too, if you want."

"Do I need to feed her something else?"

"She's a pig. She'd be twice her size if I let her eat everything she wanted."

Maddie placed one hand on the horse's head, then reached around and stroked her neck. "It's so smooth. Not soft, exactly—just very smooth. But you can really feel the muscles beneath the skin." She turned to Boone. "Is it okay if I scratch behind her ears?"

"Yeah. Fancy likes it. Slow Dance hates it."

"Will you ride him today?"

"No. I'll stay on the ground. Anyway, it's a bad idea to ride a stallion around a mare."

"Is she—" Abruptly, Maddie stopped, embarrassed.

Boone grinned broadly. "In season? No. But stallions like to show who's boss. They like to round up their herds, and you don't need the distraction. He'd be ordering Fancy around, and we need her to pay attention to you."

Just then, the mare swung her head toward Maddie's. Reflexively, Maddie jumped back.

"It's okay. She's paying attention to you. Just move slowly around her. It's always a good idea to move slowly and to stay where a horse can see you. If you're going into the blind spot behind her, make sure the horse knows where you are by keeping a constant touch on her.'' He walked toward the horse's tail. ''I'm going to walk behind her, but I'm going to let her know where I am by touching her hindquarters. See?''

Maddie watched him move to the other side of the horse and face her across the saddle. Fancy shifted, and Maddie stepped back, then frowned at herself.

''It's all right. It's good to have a healthy respect for a horse. They're big animals, and they can really hurt you. But they also feel your fear, and it will upset them. Horses are flight animals—their instinct is to run from a threat. Try to take a deep breath and reach for calm.''

''Like I do with my yoga?''

One side of his mouth curved upward. ''Yeah. Don't know that anyone teaches yoga and riding, but yeah—that's what you're going for. Reach into yourself and find a calm place. Horses are very intuitive and sensitive to your moods. Fancy here is even-tempered most of the time, but if you're upset, she'll know it.''

Maddie closed her eyes and breathed deeply, searching for that quiet, blue mountaintop pool that she visualized while she meditated.

Not easy to reach a state of peace while Boone was around, but finally Maddie found it.

One more deep breath…and she opened her eyes.

Boone watched her. His gaze held layers. Warmth. Questions. Distrust.

And something else that she was afraid to name.

"Now move closer to her and touch her again, Maddie." His voice was low and husky.

Maddie had to close her eyes again and breathe deeply to shut out his impact. Then, without looking at him again, she stepped forward and laid one hand on Fancy's neck and the other just behind the saddle.

Boone moved around and stood behind her. Maddie could feel him all across her back.

Fancy stirred.

"Damn," Boone muttered under his breath. "Maddie, shut me out. Focus on her and forget me."

Like that was possible. But Maddie tried, using every bit of control she'd gained, remembering her yoga teacher's admonitions to pull her thoughts back in focus every time they strayed.

"Okay. Now let's get you into the saddle. Grip the saddle horn with your left hand and the cantle— that's the high part at the back—with your right. Don't worry about the reins this time—I've got them."

Maddie complied.

"Now, put your left foot in the stirrup and swing yourself upward."

Maddie tried, but Fancy shifted, and she fell backward.

"Easy, Fancy," Boone soothed. "Okay, try it again." This time, he put both hands on Maddie's hips.

Maddie tried to block out the feel of his hands. Gritting her teeth, she forgot about calm and went for speed. Up she swung and landed in the saddle. The leather creaked, and Fancy shifted, dancing under her weight.

Too many sensations assaulted Maddie at once: worry about falling off, the sense of her legs spread wide across the horse's broad back, her concern that the horse might hurt Boone. She gripped the saddle horn as if it meant salvation, tightening her legs around Fancy.

"Whoa, Fancy. Settle down, girl. Grip her with your legs, but don't jab your heels into her sides, Maddie. Settle down in the saddle." One of his hands rested on her thigh, while he held the bridle and spoke to the horse.

Maddie's gaze shifted to his; the connection was instant and electric.

After a long moment, Boone squeezed her leg once and removed his hand. "You'll be fine. A horse will seldom stand still while being mounted, but it will get less scary. Just hold on, and I'm going to walk her around, so you can get used to the sensation."

Maddie wasn't sure which emotion held sway: relief that he'd quit touching her—or sorrow at that same thing. Boone's touch both calmed and disturbed her. "Thanks," she got out. Then she straightened and grabbed hold. "I'm ready."

Boone grinned. "You won't fall off, I promise. We're just going around the pen, and we'll take it slow at first."

"I know I can trust you." And she did.

He held her gaze. ''I don't know about that, Maddie Rose,'' he said softly. ''But I won't let you fall.''

The night before rose between them. Maddie wanted to say something, but she wasn't sure what. Boone's face held a strange vulnerability that she wanted to ease, but she didn't know how.

So instead, she smiled. ''Okay. I've got some work to do to become the new Annie Oakley. We'd better get started.''

Boone laughed out loud, and Maddie's heart swelled. He needed more reasons to laugh.

Then, settling his hat on his head, he walked slightly ahead of Fancy.

And Maddie the Cowgirl began a new adventure.

The next evening, Boone walked in and saw Maddie hobbling across the kitchen floor. He'd forbidden her to ride today, warning her last night that the soreness would last a couple of days and not to push it. She hadn't liked it, but he hoped that now she understood why.

It was painful to watch her.

''Here,'' he said, taking her place at the stove. ''Let me do that.''

He should have known better. Her chin jutted and her eyes shot sparks. ''I may be crippled, but I'm not helpless.''

''Maddie, go take a long hot bath and let it soothe your muscles. I can eat a sandwich.''

''I already took two today.'' Mutinous eyes dared him to poke fun.

"Wait right here." He went into Vondell's treasure trove of medicines and emerged with a yellow plastic container. He handed it to Maddie.

"What's this?"

"It's Vondell's magic potion for sore muscles. I suspect it's got horse liniment in it, but she figured out some way to not make it sting so bad or smell so rank." Then he had second thoughts. "Your skin may be too tender to use it, though. Just try a little and see what happens."

"Thank you."

"Now, tell me what I can do to help you with supper, so you can go work on those muscles."

"It's almost finished. You can set the table if you want."

When the meal was ready, Boone watched her lower herself gingerly into her chair. "You still think you want to ride again tomorrow?"

Maddie's head lifted, grin rueful. "Yes and no."

He couldn't help grinning back. "You did fine for a beginner."

"Really?"

Delight came so easily to her. She had no idea how seductive it was. He nodded. "You'll be a good rider. You're naturally graceful, and you've got a good seat already."

"It must be the yoga. I'm very limber."

He had noticed. And tried not to think of all the ways those long legs could wrap around him. Before his thoughts could escape to his face, he concentrated on his plate.

Everything fell quiet, so it was easy to hear Maddie's tiny whimper when she shifted in her chair.

Boone looked up to see her toying with her food. "Go on upstairs and take another hot bath—and use the liniment. I'll take care of the kitchen."

"All right. Thank you."

He watched her walk away as if something might break any second, and he admired her pluck. Maddie was not a complainer. And she would be a good rider, but she had work to do first. Only time would tell if she would stick with it. A day like this might have changed her mind.

Half an hour later, Boone ascended the stairs, telling himself that he was only going to take her a bottle of aspirin. The bathroom door stood ajar, the scent of Maddie's soaps and lotions drifting through the moist air. He almost turned back at the thought of Maddie lying naked in the heated water.

"Maddie?" He'd just tell her where the aspirin was and then head for the front porch.

"I'm in here." Her room, not the bathroom, thank God. "I—I think this liniment might work, but—"

He approached her room cautiously, not sure what to do. "Are you doing all right?"

"Kind of." Her voice was tight and thready.

"Are you decent?"

"Yes."

Boone peered through the opening and had to muffle a laugh. Maddie stood in her room in a bathrobe like nothing he'd ever seen; a mass of purple fabric that swallowed her up. Her back was to him, and it was covered with an explosion of color forming a peacock that extended from her shoulders down to her legs. It was the loudest damn robe he'd ever seen, but somehow it fit Maddie's colorful personality to a tee.

But his laughter was quickly stifled by the urge to groan when he watched one long, silky leg emerge from beneath the fabric.

"Oh—" She turned and saw him, and the twisted agony on her face stopped him cold. "I—I can reach everything, but—" She stood like a doe caught in a hunter's scope.

"What's wrong?"

Her face was tight. "A cramp. I bent to rub some into the back of this leg and—" Her voice showed the strain. He'd had leg cramps before—there were few things more painful.

"Here—show me where it is."

"You don't have to—" But her voice was small and uncertain, her face white with pain.

"I'll leave if you want, but it's hard to rub out a cramp in your hamstring on your own." After the other night, he didn't want to put his hands on her—yet he wanted nothing more. But Maddie was in pain, and there was no one else to help. He could control his response to her.

He knelt beside her, and he could see the muscle bunched and knotting. With a hand that trembled more than he wanted to admit, he reached out to touch the skin that he thought of too often.

It was indeed satin. But Maddie was in pain, and he couldn't think about that now.

"Lie down on your stomach."

Her hands were clenched, her teeth digging into her lower lip. With a small, shaky breath, she nodded and complied.

Boone stood up and slid the robe up out of the way—until he saw the sweet curve of her bottom revealed. His gut knotted. She was naked beneath the robe. He wanted to run from the room before he did something stupid.

But Maddie's thoughts were on anything but lust right now, and he had to control his. He dipped his fingers into the liniment and rubbed it between his hands. Drawing a deep breath, he steeled himself to touch her again.

It helped to stare across the room and knead her muscles by touch. Maddie sucked in a breath, and he responded as he would to any being in pain. "Sh-h-h, breathe slowly and try to relax," he soothed, using the voice he used with the horses, the one that calmed and reassured. "It's coming…it'll just take a minute. Breathe through the pain. Slow and steady now. That's my girl."

His back ached from bending over so far, so he settled on the bed beside her, concentrating everything he had on slow, careful motions…working the knot out, little by little.

The edges of it began to soften, and he heard Maddie sigh as the knot finally let go. Knowing that it could rebound, he kept with the motions, moving from the one spot to cover the whole leg. As his fingers slid over the back of the knee, Maddie moaned a catchy little breath. Boone moved past the sensitive spot and down to her shapely calf, then down farther to knead her long, slender foot.

Maddie sighed, and Boone smiled, glad to be easing her pain. He turned his attentions to the other foot, then up that right leg. With every stroke of his hands, Maddie melted and relaxed.

Until he reached her right thigh, and she moaned.

But it was not a moan of pain.

Boone froze, hands wrapped around her thigh. He tried to swallow, but his throat had turned to sand. Carefully, he lifted his hands from Maddie's body, and placed them on his legs, preparing to rise and leave.

"Thank you," Maddie said dreamily, her husky voice even lower, its timbre reaching down to vibrate in his loins. She rolled over, brushing hair out of her face with a lazy feline grace. Her robe gapped at the neck, and he could see the shadowy curve of one breast.

She saw where he was looking. Color was high in her cheeks, but her eyes were dark and knowing. Slender fingers dropped the satin fall of hair and moved to close the robe, her every move tempting him to stay her hand and replace it with his own.

For a moment of eternity, neither one moved.

The air crackled around them. Boone saw his own raging hunger reflected in Maddie's eyes.

He dug his fingers into denim, denying them access to what he craved. And he wanted Maddie like he'd never wanted anyone before her.

"Boone—" she began.

He could have her now. She was here, and she was willing. If only...

*No.*

He laid one finger across her lips, and that one simple touch seared his skin, shot fire through his blood. "Don't. Don't say it. Don't open that door, Maddie."

"Maybe—"

He shook his head. "No. Don't settle for less than you deserve."

Her eyes widened at that. A tiny frown appeared between her brows.

Before he could relent, before his control completely broke, Boone lifted his finger from her soft, tempting lips and rose from Maddie's bed. Drawing on every ounce of his control, he walked away from a woman who wanted him, too.

He walked away, knowing that he had done the right thing.

But when he looked back and saw her curled into a ball on the bed, it was hard to remember why doing the right thing was so important.

## Chapter Eight

Maddie rocked on the porch swing and drank her coffee, watching the sky lighten from the sunrise on the opposite side of the house. She huddled deeper into her peacock robe and wondered how she'd ever survive the next three weeks.

Her sleep had been restless though her soreness was much better, thanks to Boone's care. But another ache had replaced the twinge of ill-used muscles.

She had no name for this ache, rooted in the memory of his touch on her skin. Those hands had felt even better than she'd imagined—strong, gentle…drawing a different ache from deep down inside her. Maddie shivered at the memory. Once the knotted muscles had let go, the pain had fallen in the wake of a desire so powerful that it had knocked Maddie breathless.

She would have welcomed him into her bed at that moment and forsaken every ounce of sense she'd ever possessed. She would have opened her body to him—and paid the piper later.

But Boone had turned her down. Maddie wasn't sure how she'd ever face him again. He didn't know that it was unlike her. She had never offered herself to a man before, never come close to pleading, yet twice now she had wanted nothing more. She was still shocked at how easy it would have been to do just that.

And Boone had wanted her, too. That much, she knew. Even if she'd been blind and deaf, if she hadn't seen his eyes go dark and hot or heard his voice turn husky, Maddie would still have felt the air vibrate with electric, roaring hunger.

But Boone had had the control that she had lacked, and Maddie was still puzzling over his last words: *Don't settle for less than you deserve.*

Now she heard him on the stairs and held her breath, praying that he wouldn't see her out here, wouldn't come near.

When his steps headed away toward the kitchen, Maddie exhaled her relief. Boone could get his own breakfast this morning.

She'd been sorely tempted to pack up and leave in the middle of the night. But if she did, she would never be able to keep the promise she'd made to her father's restless spirit. She'd never satisfy her own growing yearning to know her roots. And she couldn't break her promise to Boone, though she no longer kidded herself that she'd be welcome here once her term was up.

Maddie considered her naiveté in thinking she and Boone could be friends. Right now, she didn't see how she could even be in the same room with him.

But she would do it, somehow. She wouldn't tuck tail and run. Her father had found the courage to leave all that he loved and make a new life. Her grandmother had endured dying alone. If Sam was right, her forebears had faced drought and disaster, had survived the threat of starvation. Maddie would not be found lacking just because she was embarrassed.

She wanted to give up today's riding lesson, but she wouldn't. She would face Boone somehow and keep going. Maddie Rose Collins wasn't a quitter.

But she would never let such lapses happen again. She had been right about Boone's hands: they were dangerous, so strong and skilled. She had been in such pain, and he had soothed her, had used his voice to reassure and his hands to heal. When the pain had let go, his touch had scatter-shot desire through her body. The memory of it made her shiver still.

When she heard the back door close and Boone's steps head down the porch and away, Maddie sighed.

Twenty-three days and counting.

* * *

That afternoon, Boone watched Maddie dismount, thankful that those long legs did the trick. He'd stood back and let her mount by herself earlier, not willing to risk touching her unless absolutely necessary. She'd settled into the saddle and pointedly ignored him.

An unvoiced warning had surrounded her all day. *Keep away.*

Maddie's voice could have shouted it, but her posture made that unnecessary. She had brought him lunch as had become her habit, but nothing else was the same. Instead of peppering him with questions, her laughter quick and easy, Maddie had barely looked at him. Silent as a wraith, she had only spoken to tell him that she would be ready for her next lesson whenever he had time. The fact that she even wanted to try surprised him.

It was obvious that she didn't understand why he'd pulled away from her last night, but nothing could be served by explaining. He had exactly the result he needed: Maddie had become a stranger again. Unfortunately, this time, one who didn't smile.

He should be happy. He had the distance he needed.

He *was* happy, damn it.

Muttering a dark oath, Boone dismounted from Gulliver. He and Maddie had passed the time silently, each lost in their own thoughts. Conversation had been limited to what he'd needed to say to guide her on proper handling of her horse. Maddie's responses had been short and to the point. Not rude or angry, just—

Not Maddie.

*Keep away.* He hadn't realized how much he'd miss her sparkle.

He heard a car come up the road and stop in front of the house. Glancing at Maddie, he saw that she didn't recognize it, either.

''Want me to see who it is, or stay with the horses?'' she asked.

The day was too hot. He'd unsaddle the horses first. ''You go ahead. I'll be right there.''

Boone made short work of unsaddling the horses and turning them out. With long strides he made his way to the house.

When he opened the back door, he heard the sound he'd been missing.

Maddie's laughter.

The black-haired man looked up from his glass of tea, green eyes sliding from laughter to wariness.

''Boone,'' Maddie said, ''this is Devlin Marlowe.''

Marlowe rose and held out his hand. He was a few inches shorter than Boone, lean but with an air of muscles waiting to explode into motion. He reminded Boone of a boxer, and his nose attested to at least one break. But he hadn't taken many blows to the head if he did box—his eyes held keen intelligence, looking at Boone with too much knowledge.

''Boone Gallagher,'' he replied, responding to Marlowe's firm grip with his own.

Then they stepped back to their corners and each studied the other.

"Would you like some iced tea, Boone?" Maddie asked.

He jerked his gaze away and nodded. "I can get it."

Maddie's tone turned formal when speaking to him. "Just sit down. I have a glass right here." She handed Boone his tea, then turned to Marlowe, offering the pitcher with a smile. "More tea, Mr. Marlowe?"

"Thank you. Please call me Dev, Ms. Collins."

Maddie's smile brightened. "Oh, let's don't stand on ceremony, Dev. Call me Maddie." She turned to Boone and her eyes gleamed. "Dev was in my restaurant once, he tells me."

Marlowe's smile widened. "Best food I ever put in my mouth."

"What did you have?" she asked.

They began discussing the menu as if there was nothing more important in life than fine food. It irritated the hell out of Boone how the two of them smiled and laughed like old friends.

He cleared his throat. "What do you need to look at here to find my brother?"

Marlowe looked a little startled at the brusque interruption, and cast a quick, apologetic smile at Maddie. "Anything you've got. I don't always know until I see it. Your father just handed me what he thought I needed."

The mention of Sam strained the atmosphere.

Boone wondered exactly what his father had told this man about him. Nothing very good, from Marlowe's manner toward him.

It didn't matter. Sam was dead, and it was none of Marlowe's business what had happened between Boone and his father.

"We'll go through his office first, then you might want to go through the attic. There used to be boxes of stuff up there. I don't know if there's anything that could help you, but my mother never threw anything away—even things that were here when we moved in."

Maddie's quick gasp caught his attention. "Before you moved in? You mean, there might be something of my grandmother's up there?"

Boone nodded slowly, sorry that he hadn't remembered them before. "I think I remember a trunk or something that was in the attic when we first started putting stuff up there."

Maddie looked ready to race up the stairs that very minute.

Boone held up a hand. "Maddie, I don't know if Sam kept any of it."

Maddie rose. "I'd like to see."

"It's too hot up there right now, in this afternoon heat. I wouldn't recommend either of you going up until morning."

"What about tonight when it cools down?"

"There's no electricity up there."

"What about a flashlight?"

"I don't know how good the footing is, but there's a big window if you can wait until morning."

Impatience jittered in Maddie's expression.

Marlowe spoke up. "I second Boone. I've had to crawl through attics more than once. The heat is usually at least ten degrees higher than outside, and it's already a hundred degrees today. You're talking heatstroke."

She subsided, clearly disappointed.

"What are you looking for?" Boone asked.

"Anything I can find that would tell me something about my grandmother or my father."

"I'll show you what I've gathered in my files, Maddie," Marlowe offered.

She turned a grateful smile on him, the wattage blinding.

*He's her kind, Boone. He comes from her world, the world you made Helen leave.* Boone could see the writing on the wall. Marlowe would find Mitch. Maddie would gratefully return to her life. Hell, they might even wind up in New York together, for all he knew.

The thought turned his voice curt. "I'll show you Sam's files, Marlowe. Then I've got to get back to the barn."

"You'll stay for dinner, Dev?" Maddie asked.

Marlowe beamed. "You're cooking?"

She nodded.

He turned to Boone. "This woman is feeding you? Do you know how lucky you are? A top-notch chef here in Morning Star, cooking in your kitchen?''

For some reason, Boone remembered radish roses. He glanced at Maddie, seeing her as the outside world knew her instead of as a barefoot woman in cutoffs with flour on her cheek.

And he realized that he'd been a fool to entertain the idea that there would ever be a decision for Maddie to make. She wasn't the woman who'd been living here with him, who petted calves and swung on the porch. That woman was an illusion, as is any person who's on vacation, assuming a persona that isn't real.

He'd never even met the real Maddie Collins.

With the force of a sledgehammer, it hit Boone that somewhere deep inside he'd been harboring the tiny seed of a dream.

A shaken Boone turned. ''I have to get back to work. The files are this way.''

With a determined step, Boone crushed the tiny seed into powder.

Maddie stared out the kitchen window at the still-dark sky, her coffee cooling while her thoughts tumbled, unable to land on anything but how much she wished the sunlight would hurry.

Above her, she heard Boone's steps heading for the shower. She glanced at the clock, judging when to put the biscuits into the oven. She'd been up for two hours. Boone might not want anything she'd cooked, but she'd needed to stay busy.

Too bad Dev hadn't accepted their offer to stay here last night. At least he would talk to her—unlike Boone, who had reverted to the silent stranger she had first met.

Too bad Dev wasn't the person she really wanted to know.

It was better this way, though. Hearing Dev's enthusiastic response to her food—even when she didn't have access to the ingredients she would have liked—had reminded Maddie that there was a whole world of people out there who would welcome her back from Nowhere, Texas. Maybe it was only because of her cooking, but that was all right.

She knew people. She would be fine.

But Boone would stay here, locked in his self-imposed prison. He could die an old man here, never venturing farther than fifty miles away.

*Stop being fanciful, Maddie.* Boone was a grown man who had traveled the world. He would find someone to marry. He would have children. He would be just fine.

But something deep inside Maddie knew differently. And she ached for the man who had taken a couple of steps toward his freedom...until the other night.

Now he had slammed the prison door shut again. The Boone who had begun to smile just a little was long gone.

And Maddie missed him—

The shower shut off.

In response, Maddie shut off her thoughts. She

had one priority right now: finding out about her family.

Maddie opened the oven door and placed the biscuits inside.

Boone smelled bread baking and groaned inwardly. No slipping out of the house without seeing her this morning. When he entered the kitchen, he could see the restless night in her eyes. He nodded and headed for the coffee.

"Two eggs or three?" she asked.

His back turned to her, he sipped carefully. "Maddie, I told you not—"

"I couldn't sleep. The sun isn't up yet. Humor me."

He faced her, studying the lines of strain on her face. "Finding something in the attic means a lot to you, doesn't it?"

She nodded. "Two eggs or three?"

"Three. But there might not be anything up there."

She shrugged. "If there isn't, there isn't. But I have to look. I won't prowl through your family's belongings any more than I must to find my grandmother's things."

Boone frowned. "I don't care about that." But he did care about her almost certain heartache. Sam might not have kept any of it. And anyway, Boone had no idea what had been in the trunk he thought he'd seen so long ago.

"Do you want me to wait for Dev?" she asked.

"Do you think you need a chaperone?"

A quick smile curved her lips. "I think I can behave."

His own lips twitched slightly. "I doubt that, but go ahead."

Maddie lifted her head, her gaze searching his. Boone realized that it was the first time she'd really looked at him since the other night.

"Are you teasing me, Boone? You?"

Abruptly, he sobered. "Maddie, I don't want you getting your hopes up. There might be nothing there."

"There will be. I can feel it. I know I'll find something." Boone almost sighed—he'd forgotten the flaky gypsy. Her chin tilted upward. "I'm just curious, that's all."

She was lying. Everything about her spoke of nerves this morning. "Do you want me to go up there with you?"

"Why?"

*So I can protect you from what you might find. Or not find.* He shrugged. "The boxes might be heavy."

For a long span she studied him, the silver eyes softening to gray velvet. "I'll be all right. I'll come get you if there's something too heavy." With practiced ease, she dished up his eggs and pulled the biscuits from the oven, piling four on his plate.

His hand reached for the plate. She held on, their gazes meeting. "Thank you," she said softly.

Boone couldn't take his eyes off her.

Finally Maddie let go. Boone reminded himself of

what was real. What was possible. With a nod, he headed for the table.

Maddie climbed the attic stairs, grateful that Dev had called to say it would be this afternoon before he could return, and that he'd just deal with Sam's desk then to see if he even needed to search the attic. She really wanted to do this alone, to seek her grandmother's spirit in a way that she could never do if accompanied by a stranger.

Her heart thumped heavily in her chest with every step.

Then she reached the top and just stared.

Across the large attic, motes floated in the air, turned golden by the rays of the morning sun. The narrow path between boxes was floored with broad wooden planks, undisturbed under a blanket of years of dust. She smelled the slightly mildewed scent of old fabrics and cardboard. With delight, Maddie filled her lungs—and then coughed.

*Such a romantic.* But she couldn't help smiling, eagerly anticipating treasures in this place.

And treasures there were—but none of them her grandmother's. She found a box labeled in loopy feminine handwriting, Boone's Baby Clothes. Her fingers itched to open its flaps. *I don't care about that.* She remembered Boone's words. Carefully, she pried open just one flap.

On top lay a pair of tiny brown cowboy boots stitched in yellow and red, so small that the soles barely covered her hand. Beneath, she could see little garments, but Maddie ventured no further. It wasn't her right, no matter how longing squeezed her heart. These things belonged to Boone and his future wife. And to his children.

With careful fingers, Maddie closed the box, trying not to think of a little boy with Boone's golden hair and blue eyes…and moved on.

Bless Jenny Gallagher for her careful labeling—box after box marked Keepsakes 1966 or Mitch's Toys. Maddie wondered if Boone had any idea what a wealth of memories lay up here.

A few boxes lay on top, unmarked and jumbled in piles. Maddie opened them carefully but could immediately tell that they held papers related to the ranch. Sam must have stuck them up here—instead of being carefully folded and packed, these items seemed almost thrown into boxes, not one of which was labeled.

Maddie scoured the attic, lifting box after box, some of them heavy enough that she should have called Boone to help. But she wanted to find Rose's things in private. She reached the single window at the far end and looked behind her, realizing that she'd almost covered the attic.

And found nothing.

Her heart clutched. Boone had warned her, but she had hoped.

Oh, how she had hoped.

She swept the flashlight beam across the expanse, trying to be sure she'd covered it all. An odd shape beneath an old torn, yellowed sheet caught her eye.

Carefully, Maddie picked her way through the boxes, heart pounding as she removed the obstacles in her way. She barked her shin on one sharp corner but hardly minded, so intent was she upon reaching her last hope.

Her fingers trembled as she tugged at the sheet and heard the rip of worn fabric. Maddie drew a deep breath and struggled to be calm and careful. With the steps of a penitent approaching the throne, Maddie moved closer.

It was a very old trunk, the leather cracked with the passage of years, the brass tarnished. Maddie closed her eyes and prayed that it wasn't locked.

It was. She looked around, fighting the urge to cry.

She'd always said that she was a good hand with a knife. Hoping Vondell would forgive her, Maddie climbed down the steps and retrieved an assortment of kitchen implements.

She didn't care, long minutes later, that her hair was glued to her neck with sweat. All that mattered was that she'd heard a click and that the latch had popped open.

Shaking like a leaf, Maddie lifted the lid and looked inside. The faint smell of lavender and moth-balls teased her nose. Another yellowed sheet lay over the contents. Maddie lifted it carefully and set it aside.

On the left side lay a stack of books and things; on the right, a pile of fabric—clothing, she guessed.

Maddie lifted a black leather scrapbook in her hands, afraid to open it.

Drawing a deep breath, she took a look. On the front page was the hand-lettered name: Dalton.

Maddie's heart stuttered. She'd found it. On page two, she saw the tiny dark curl of hair carefully placed inside an envelope turned yellow with the years. On the outside, it read, Dalton's first haircut, age two.

Maddie ran one reverent finger over the lock of her father's baby hair. When a tear dropped on the page, she jerked her head up, swiping at her eyes. She wouldn't do anything to harm this precious evidence.

*It all belongs to you, Maddie Rose.* She could almost hear her father's voice. With a shock, it truly hit her. These things were hers now. She was the last of her line: the last Wheeler.

Maddie Rose Wheeler. Was that who she was? And where did she belong?

Maddie lost track of time as she thumbed through the album, seeing her father grow from infancy to boyhood to football team member in high school. In his childish face, she could see some of her own features. And in the very few teenage photos, she could see the beginnings of the man she'd known.

She almost thought that she could see the beginning of the end, the time when Rose had let Buster Caswell and his poison into their lives. Dalton stopped smiling as life grew more solemn. She couldn't bear to think of what had been happening to them then.

Some of the photos had been taken at this very house, on the porch outside. She saw her father riding a pony near a barn that she recognized, and suddenly she was struck by a pain so sharp she that gasped aloud.

This ranch held her past. How could she walk away from all that they had loved?

But she heard Boone's voice: *You can't mean to stay.* She remembered his eyes, revealing how much he needed this place.

*Please, Daddy, Grandmother Rose. I can't stay. Please understand.*

*But I won't forget.*

Maddie laid down the album and made a mental note to ask Boone to help her carry the trunk downstairs. Then she reached inside for the large cloth item that took up most of the right side. Unfolding it carefully, Maddie cried out as she realized what it was.

A wedding dress. Inside its folds lay a picture of a woman Maddie knew in an instant was her grandmother Rose.

She knew because she might have been looking in a mirror.

Maddie's eyes filled with tears as she devoured the sight of a tall man who had her father's build and his dark hair, standing beside a woman who looked for all the world like Maddie Rose. The woman was dressed in this very same gown, with its simple cut, the lace now yellowed with age.

Her knees shaky and weak, Maddie stood and set the picture down with care. She backed away into the small open space and held up the dress, trying to imagine what it would look like on her. With careful steps, she pressed it to her body and closed her eyes.

*Oh, Grandmother, how I wish I'd known you.*

That was how Boone found her. He'd come inside, since Maddie hadn't appeared at her usual time. He'd intended only to make a quick sandwich and go back to work, but the day was hot and he'd begun to worry. Deciding to check and make sure she hadn't passed out from the heat, he'd mounted the stairs, assuming she'd hear his steps.

When he reached the top, he couldn't speak. Maddie stood in the sunlight, holding an ivory gown against her, her eyes closed and tears rolling down her cheeks.

With careful steps, Boone crossed to her. "Maddie?" he spoke softly.

Her eyes opened, showing him a world of such pain and confusion that he reached for her without considering anything but that she needed to be held.

Maddie was always so relentlessly cheerful that he'd come to think nothing could bring her down. To see that he was so very wrong struck him in a way that scattered his resolutions. Maddie needed someone. Right now, it would have to be him.

She nestled into him and sobbed softly. Boone thought at that instant that he would slay dragons to bring back Maddie's smile.

"Why couldn't I know her, Boone? Why did I miss so much?"

He had no answers, no way to change the past. So he just held her while she cried.

After a moment, her face turned up to his. In her eyes he saw such need for comfort, such loneliness and despair, that he did something he knew he would regret.

He kissed her.

He only meant it to comfort, to ease her pain, to let her know that she wasn't alone. But one touch was all it took. One brush of lips…and he was lost.

Maddie slid one arm out from between them and gripped his shirt in one fist, lifting herself to her tiptoes, bringing back the hunger that had never really left him.

Boone forgot about good intentions, forgot about being the wrong man. Forcing himself to go slowly, he licked softly at her full lower lip and heard her intake of breath. A quick prickling heat flashed through him, raising the hairs on the back of his neck. For one instant, an instinct as old as man warned him away, reminded him of danger.

Then Maddie parted her lips and her tongue stroked him back, her fingers pressing into his side, her breasts soft against his chest.

He had to get closer. With one hand he gripped the back of her head, sliding his fingers into the thick fall of dark hair and turning her into his kiss. His tongue slid into the sweetness of Maddie's mouth, and he wanted to stay there forever, to drink of her kind heart, to revive her cheerful soul, to soothe her despair and her sorrow.

Maddie knew only that Boone was here, sharing his strength when she couldn't find her own, that he warmed the cold corners of her anguish and made her feel, for the first time in years, that she wasn't alone.

His kiss was a balm and a solace, but it was so much more. In his kiss, Maddie found a dark, edgy promise of excitement, of bliss beyond the power of words. Maddie felt the ragged border of Boone's own anguish, and she poured herself into soothing him, forgetting her own pain as she touched the rawness of Boone's grief.

He was so strong that he hid his pain too well, but for a moment Maddie thought she knew his heart's need. She lifted herself higher, sliding her fingers into his hair, murmuring soothing comfort. But it was mingled with sharp spikes of need.

Through Boone shot the same fierce need to possess her that had driven him the night of the dance. He dropped his hands lower and gripped her hips. Pulling her hard against him, he wanted to tear off her clothes and his own, to salve this endless ache that was so much more than physical.

Maddie felt the strength of his arousal. His hand slid upward and cupped her breast. She arched against him, pressing into his palm.

When his fingers tightened, Maddie bucked against him. She felt her grandmother's dress slipping from nerveless fingers. It was then that she realized how close she'd danced to the edge of a terrifying precipice.

It was one second of sanity in a world gone mad with longing.

One second of hesitation, facing the point of no return.

Could she do this to him? To herself? For a moment, Maddie flirted with the idea of staying, of yielding to the ever-increasing sense of connection to this place, to the past—

To this man.

The second's pause was fatal to something too new, too fragile. It gave Boone time to feel her doubts. To remember.

He couldn't let himself need Maddie. He couldn't let her in this close. She spoke to him on a level deeper than anyone in his life had ever gone.

Shaken to his boots, he realized that Maddie could break him, when nothing else in his life ever had.

She felt him leave her, felt him pull away just the tiniest bit. It might as well have been the Grand Canyon.

She dangled over the precipice, raw and needy. Alone again for one eternal moment when she had thought she'd found home.

Why hadn't she learned from the past? Robert had brought her down, but he had been nothing like Boone, had not wielded a fraction of Boone's power to hurt her. Boone was a thousand times more dangerous to everything she'd been trying to recover.

Boone wanted her—yes. She even thought he needed her.

But he didn't *want* to want her. And he needed her gone.

Maddie stepped back, her chest heaving.

Boone didn't stop her, though his empty fingers flexed and his chest ached.

Maddie couldn't look at Boone, couldn't bear to see the truth on his face. One hand pressed tightly to her lips, she turned away and grabbed up her grandmother's dress, holding it to her breast. She stared out the window.

She started to speak, but her voice wasn't hers to command. Maddie cleared her throat and tried again.

"I found my grandmother's things."

Behind her, she heard his voice, low and strained. "I see that. Do you want me to carry the trunk downstairs to your room?"

So polite. So distant.

"If it's not too much trouble."

"No trouble."

Maddie didn't turn around. Behind her, she heard Boone close the trunk and lift it, heading for the stairs. With a shaky breath, she turned and carefully folded the dress, wrapping it back in the sheet that she had dropped in her haste. Fighting hard to hold inside the emotions careening out of control, Maddie carried the dress down the stairs.

When she passed Boone leaving her room, she

cast one quick glance at him. If she had seen the slightest sign that he was struggling, too, she might have tried to talk to him, though she had no idea what to say.

There were no words for the power of what had passed between them.

Nor for the impossibility of what kept them apart.

But Maddie didn't have to worry. The man who had kissed her, the man whose heart had lain bare to her own for a few precious seconds—that man lay safely buried behind a mask of stone. That man might have existed only in her very vivid imagination.

For one endless second, every fiber of Maddie's soul cried out for that man's return.

## Chapter Nine

Boone closed up the attic and walked out of the house like a man gone blind. He fought an urge to get in his truck and head for the nearest port, to lose himself as an anonymous seaman once again. To hide out somewhere, anywhere, until Maddie left.

He squinted against the scorching sun and lectured the part of him that seemed bent on destruction.

She won't stay.

*You haven't asked her.*

Remember how she was with Marlowe? She can't wait to get back.

*She wasn't thinking about New York up in the attic.*

For a minute, that was all. Yes, there was heat between them. Boone shook his head. Heat, hell—there was nuclear meltdown.

But it wasn't enough. Maddie deserved so much more. And what did he have to offer? A man so bad at love that his only child never had a chance to be born? A life of hard work and loneliness stuck away in the wilderness? He'd already ruined one woman's life. He would not risk Maddie…bright, beautiful Maddie.

*You could go with her. To the city.*

No.

He could not. He would not forsake this place again. Now, more than ever, he was needed to be its guardian. For the sake of the desolation in Maddie's eyes, he would keep this place safe. It was one thing that he could do for her, no matter what his other shortcomings. He no longer expected to have a family of his own, but if Mitch didn't want the ranch, maybe Maddie's children would.

*A hell of a life, Boone ol' buddy.*

It's who I am. It's all I really need.

And with that thought, Boone straightened his hat and headed for the barn. Lunch was the last thing on his mind.

Maddie spread the dress out on her bed carefully, smoothing its folds. When she'd first held it, she'd been eager to try it on. Not anymore.

Instead, she sank down on the rug by the bed and reached into the trunk again, her movements lethargic. She looked through framed pictures of unidentified people. Maybe later she'd take them out of the frames and see if anyone had marked them on the back, but not now.

At the bottom of the pile, Maddie saw a little red leather book that looked like a diary.

With shaking fingers, she lifted it out and sat back down, cradling it on her lap. With slow strokes, she traced the shabby remains of what might once have been gold leaf. Then she drew in a deep breath and opened the cover.

Rose McCall, it said in spiky, formal script. Beneath it was added the name Wheeler, with a heart drawn beside it.

So now Maddie knew. Her grandmother's maiden name had been McCall. And she had loved Jack Wheeler, the grandfather who had died too soon. Rose might even have been a romantic, Maddie thought. Drawing the heart was something a younger Maddie might have done.

The thought of her grandmother as a hopeful young bride brought a smile. Then Maddie remembered how it had all turned out, and her heart ached for the woman she'd never met.

Reining in her thoughts, Maddie turned the page. The diary seemed to start when Rose was twelve, and soon Maddie was lost in a life utterly different from anything she'd known. Rose spoke of hard times, and Maddie found a date that pinpointed this as what came to be called the Great Depression. But Rose spoke of girlish dreams and seemed to take the hardships in stride.

Soon Maddie traveled with Rose through teenage

years in a world so innocent that it was hard to believe. She marveled at the simplicity of life, the lack of cynicism, the focus on a world close at hand.

Until Maddie's stomach growled, she never even registered that she'd forgotten to eat lunch. A quick glance at the shifted sunlight told her that lunch was hours past. Reluctantly, she closed the book and reached for the table to set it down, but she didn't reach far enough, and it slipped off the table's edge. As she grabbed for it, a folded sheet of paper fluttered to the floor.

Maddie righted the book and opened the paper. The sheet bore no date. Maddie read the words on the page with growing disbelief.

I do not know what to do. I have just heard that Jenny is marrying Sam Gallagher. My heart cries out to tell her that Dalton is not dead, but what good would it do? I curse the day I cast all of our lives into hell by fighting back when Buster raged. Now I have no son, and Jenny is marrying another. My son is lost to me. He paid too high a price to save me. If I knew where he was, I would turn myself in so that he could reclaim his life, no matter what Ben says.

I am the last of my line. My blood will not inherit this place.

My mind returns, again and again, to Jenny's visit before she left town months ago. She was pale and trembling; she would start to speak as if to confide, then lapse into silence. It was all

I could do to cling to the story that Dalton was dead.

She has been gone for seven months. I think back to cues that were there and wonder. Did Jenny bear my grandchild somewhere far away? Is there a piece of my son lost to us all?

And do I have the right to ask her? I could be wrong. It could be wishful thinking. Jenny was always an upright child, but she did love Dalton deeply, as he loved her. They could have yielded to natural urges. But once he vanished, would she not have told me or asked me for help?

Perhaps not. She was always a thoughtful girl, and she knew I was half out of my mind with grief.

Sam is a good young man, Dalton's best friend. But I have known for years that he loved Jenny, too, though she never had eyes for anyone but my son. If she had borne Dalton's child, would Sam have taken it to his heart? And what would it do to their fledgling marriage if I bring my questions to light?

I must think on this longer, and pray for guidance. Jenny has suffered greatly. I do not wish to cause her more pain. I cannot offer her the comfort of hearing that Dalton is alive without torturing her with the knowledge that he is lost to us both. Ben told him he had to vanish and make a new life under a new name. Even Ben doesn't know where he is now.

Ben is a good man who has helped me carry a heavy secret. He is happy for his Sam to be marrying Jenny. After all he has done for Dalton and me, do I have the right to destroy Sam's happiness?

I do not know the answers. Dear Lord, guide me in the right path.

Maddie didn't know what to think, how to feel. She flipped the diary open to the last page. It was dated a year earlier. She had been through the entire trunk. There was nowhere else to look for the answer to Rose's questions.

Then it hit her. She might have a brother or sister out there somewhere. She might not be alone, after all. Her pulse scrambled.

Where were the answers? What would Boone say when she told him?

Oh, dear. Boone. If there had been a child of Jenny and Dalton's, it would be his half sibling, too....

But Boone thought his mother an angel. And Boone had had so much uproar in his life lately. Did she have the right to destroy his image of her, too—the one thing left pure and shining from his childhood?

Maddie knew only too well how it felt to suddenly find out that your parent wasn't the person you thought. She couldn't put Boone through that with so little evidence. She couldn't tell Boone until she was sure. What she'd read was pure speculation on Rose's part, guessing that her son had—

Maddie sat down heavily. Had fathered a child he'd never even known he had. With the woman he had loved first and best. Her eyes filled with tears. So much loss, so much pain. Maddie ached for one more example of all her father had sacrificed, even if he'd never known it.

Then excitement stirred again. She might have a brother or sister—she couldn't wait to find him or her. She leapt to her feet and prepared to race down to the telephone to call—

Whom? She had no one who would understand but Boone.

Then she remembered. Dev would be back. Dev would help her.

She had to keep this from Boone until she knew whether or not this child even existed. Then she would figure out a way to break the news.

Maybe he would be happy. It would be a piece of his mother, lost for years.

But even as Maddie voiced the thought in her mind, she knew she might be very wrong. She was alone. She had reason to welcome a sibling. Boone already had a brother and a clear, untarnished image of his mother in his mind.

Maddie would not disturb that fragile memory. Not yet, not until there was no choice. It was the least she could do for a man whose life had already been thrown into chaos by other people's mistakes.

\* \* \*

Boone was out in the north pasture digging post holes when Jim found him.

"You plannin' to dig your way down to China?"

Boone kept working, needing the exertion. The handles of the post hole diggers held tight in his fists, he struck another harsh blow into the soil, until the clang of metal against limestone sent a shock singing up his arms.

"It's getting late. You about ready to wrap up?"

Boone shot Jim a glance. Without speaking, he shook his head.

"A little tough to dig post holes in the dark," Jim observed casually.

Boone jammed the post hole diggers down in the hole and jerked around. "What the hell do you want, Jim?"

"It won't help, you know."

"We already agreed that this fence needs moving."

"This fall. Not today. And you know that's not what I'm talking about."

Boone paused then, staring off into the distance.

"Three weeks left, right?"

Boone nodded.

"You gonna waste them digging post holes, or you gonna see if that little gal might change her mind and stay here?"

"She won't." Boone's jaw tightened.

Jim cursed, long and low. "You asked her, flat out?"

"No. But she's said it often enough."

"You could change her mind. I've seen her look at you."

He shot Jim a glance. "What do you mean by that?"

"After the dance, she looked at you like some kind of hero."

A thousand years had passed between him and Maddie since the dance. A thousand miles they'd traveled on a path leading nowhere.

"Leave it alone, Jim. There's no future for Maddie and me."

"So you're just going to leave it at that? There's nothing left of the boy inside the man?"

Boone's head jerked up. "What does that mean?"

"I knew a fourteen-year-old boy who kept this ranch from going under through sheer will, when everything else in his life had fallen to pieces."

"I had you to help me. And I left as soon as I could."

"Four years later. Four years of hell. And anyone would have left. You came back when Sam needed you, even though he'd treated you like something he scraped off his boot."

"And I managed to kill my wife and—" Boone swore at what he'd almost revealed.

But Jim didn't notice. "You are going to beat yourself into the ground about that worthless woman until the day you die, aren't you? And in the meantime, you're going to let pure gold slip through your fingers."

"You don't understand."

"I understand that you're doing something I never thought I'd see from you. You're giving up without a fight."

"I'm trying to do right by her, damn it. There's nothing for her here." His already strained temper exploded. "You tell me why a woman who could take New York by storm would want to settle for a piece of dirt in Texas, Jim. I sure as hell can't figure it out. But you go ahead—figure out why in the hell Maddie would want to stay here, and I'll be glad to fight to keep her."

Jim looked only slightly chastened. "Maddie feels something for this place—more every day."

Boone fought the urge to rub his chest where it ached. "But it's not enough."

The older man studied him. "Maybe she's waiting for you to give her more reasons."

Boone couldn't let himself think about how much he wished that were true. And his pride kept him from telling Jim that he couldn't stand not being enough for Maddie, watching that bright light dim as she got past the sentimental attachment to her grandmother's place and realized that all he had to offer wasn't enough.

"Luanne Mason has been talking about selling The Dinner Bell."

Boone snorted. "Maddie's got job offers in Manhattan. Why would she want a greasy spoon in Morning Star?"

"Maybe there's more to Maddie than you realize.

She's been wandering for a long time. I think she's hungry for someplace to belong.''

Jim's theory was so far-fetched. Jim hadn't seen her with Marlowe, hadn't watched her eyes light up, discussing New York. But for one treacherous instant, Boone let himself think about Maddie staying. Even if The Dinner Bell only kept her here for a while, it would buy him time to bind her to him, to think of something else.

No, it was crazy. *He* was crazy for grasping at straws.

''I can tell you're already talking yourself out of it. I know it's a long shot, but when did that ever stop you before?''

It was more than a long shot. It was a trip to Mars. But there was nothing to be lost by mentioning it to Maddie, he guessed.

But was it right for Maddie?

Boone looked at the lowering sun and grabbed the post hole diggers in one hand. ''I'll mention it, even though it won't do any good.''

Satisfaction lit up Jim's grin. ''It's a start, son.''

''It's a dead end, and you know it.''

''It wouldn't be the first time Maddie surprised you.'' Jim walked away, whistling.

Jim had no idea how much Boone wished, for once, that the older man was right.

He loaded up his gear and headed for the house.


Boone walked in the back door, eager and nervous the way he hadn't been since his first date.

Then he heard a man's voice, along with Maddie's.

Oh, hell. He'd forgotten about Marlowe.

He decided to head for the shower and hope Marlowe would be gone before he got out, but as he passed Sam's office, Maddie appeared in the doorway.

"Oh—hi, Boone." Her eyes were huge and dark, her face pale. "I didn't realize—" She held the edge of the door as if she was hiding something.

Then Marlowe opened the door wide behind her, and a furtive glance passed between them.

Boone's hopes died with that glance.

A damn fool, he was, to have courted hope, even for the last few minutes. Marlowe was her type, lived in her world.

*You could live in that world, Boone.*

No, he couldn't. Not anymore. And Maddie couldn't live in his.

"Marlowe," he nodded. "Maddie."

"I haven't fixed dinner yet," she said. "I can—"

He cut her off ruthlessly. "I'm going out." Not that he knew where. Just away from here.

"Oh." Relief skipped across her features. She and Marlowe traded another glance.

Then it hit him like a fist to the gut: the memory of what it had felt like to be the man deceived. To know that the woman in your life wanted to be with someone else.

Thank God he hadn't yet told Maddie what he'd come up here thinking tonight. He hadn't laid his heart on the ground to be trampled. His pride was intact.

Funny how it didn't feel that great.

"Find everything you need, Marlowe?"

Marlowe's gaze met his with slight hesitation. "Yeah. Maddie's been helping me."

Within Boone rose a howling beast that wanted to punch the man's lights out. Wanted to smash him into a pulp, just for being right for Maddie when Boone was all wrong.

He crushed that beast down. "Good." He nodded. Then his voice turned rougher than he intended. "Find my brother, Marlowe."

He thought he saw sympathy in the man's eyes, and the beast roared out again.

Marlowe nodded. "I'm doing everything I can."

*Oh, I can see what you're doing.* Before he did something he would regret, Boone turned away and climbed the stairs.

Boone had been gone for four days, and Jim said he might make one more livestock auction before he returned. Maddie was glad. Waiting for updates from Dev was hard enough without sneaking around Boone. More than once in the two days before Boone had left, Maddie had driven into Morning Star to call Dev, afraid of accidentally revealing the quest to Boone before she had any concrete answers.

But she missed him, more than she'd ever imagined. Never mind that he'd been only a polite stranger before he left—the house felt huge and empty without him.

She'd taken to cooking for Jim and Sonny and sending meals home with them. Both men's wives had sent their thanks for the break. Velda had even told Jim that Maddie should buy The Dinner Bell and make everyone in Morning Star happy.

Maddie tried to imagine owning a place called The Dinner Bell. Tried to imagine what she would serve.

Her city friends would split their sides laughing.

But Maddie wasn't laughing. For a few insane moments, she had actually considered it seriously.

Then last night, Régine had called from Sancerre and upped the ante. She'd dangled a potential ownership interest before Maddie—a very tempting prospect.

But Régine was getting impatient. She wanted a commitment, wanted Maddie there now. Maddie had tried to explain her responsibility to Boone, but Régine couldn't seem to understand why throwing money at the problem wouldn't work. Surely the Caswells would take money to go away and let Boone have the place early.

Maddie wasn't prepared to discuss a past fraught with tragedy to a woman who couldn't care less. Nor could she truly explain why her promise to Boone was so important.

Régine had accused Maddie of falling in love with a cowboy, had teased Maddie about succumbing to a pair of tight jeans.

How could she explain Boone's haunted eyes, his nobility, the way he made her feel inside? Régine made him into a cliché, and Maddie had had to bite her tongue to avoid offending the woman who dangled a tantalizing future before her.

She wasn't in love with Boone. She couldn't afford to be. It was the road to heartache.

Boone was headed north toward Morning Star, almost to the turnoff for the ranch, when he saw Maddie's car tear onto the highway without even stopping at the intersection.

Something was wrong. She was driving like a bat out of hell. Was someone hurt? Where was she going?

He was dog tired after long days of examining stock and trying to plan out a future. And long nights when he imagined what Maddie and Marlowe were doing at the ranch while he was gone.

A part of him protested that Maddie was not like Helen, that even Helen had never flaunted her affair in his face. Another part of him dug in claws, reminding him that he had no claim on Maddie, that she and Marlowe were two of a kind. That he had no right to care what she did or didn't do in his absence.

He could have hit one more auction, but he'd done well at the ones he'd attended. He'd bought stock to build a future—one whose emptiness he didn't want to consider.

Boone wasn't sure what was harder: being with

Maddie or being without her. He missed her smile, her easy laughter. He missed the bright sparkle. He even missed her sass, damn it.

Seventeen days left before he'd have to miss her forever.

But memories reminded Boone of the furtive glances between her and Marlowe, the calls she'd hung up abruptly before he'd left, the unexplained absences—not that Maddie owed him any accounting for her whereabouts.

He had been an easy man to deceive once before. He knew that his desire for Maddie would make him an easy mark, once again.

Part of him said that Maddie was a big girl, that whatever reason she had for speeding north into town this afternoon was her own business. He was pulling a full trailer of stock behind his truck. He should turn off to the ranch.

But that wasn't the part to which Boone was listening. Maybe she was in trouble. He had to find out. He pressed down on the accelerator, knowing there wasn't a chance in hell that he could catch her. But if he was lucky, maybe he could keep her in sight. If not, Morning Star was small enough. He would find her.

Maddie stopped the car beside the basketball courts in the park, barely remembering to remove the keys in her excitement over Dev's call that he'd found something. She saw him under the trees and raced across the grass.

"You didn't have to break the land speed record," he teased.

"Tell me," she panted. "Have you found the baby? Is it real?"

Dev's face grew solemn. "Maddie—" His voice went soft.

"Don't coddle me, Dev. Tell me what you know."

"All right." Dev grasped her shoulders, his eyes twinkling. "There was a baby. Jenny left Morning Star and gave birth in Mineral Wells. She gave the baby up in a private adoption."

"A boy or girl?"

"A girl."

A sister. She had a sister. Overcome, Maddie threw her arms around Dev's neck and cried out for joy. "I have a sister, Dev. I always wanted a sister. You have no idea how much."

Dev held her awkwardly, patting her back.

Then his silence sank in. Maddie pulled back. "Where is she?"

His shoulders sagged slightly. "Maddie—" His voice held a note of warning that sent a chill to her heart.

"She's dead," Maddie said, and put one hand to her mouth.

Dev shook his head and wrapped an arm around her shoulders. "No, we don't know that. She survived birth, at least. But I don't want you to get your hopes up, Maddie. It's not going to be easy to find her."

Maddie frowned. "Why not?"

"Her birth was never recorded or where she was born. The adoption wasn't done through the system. There was an old doctor in Mineral Wells who specialized in this type of case. He delivered babies and placed them with parents who, for various reasons, did not want to go through normal channels."

"So how do you know this is Dalton and Jenny's baby?"

"The old doctor is long dead. We only have Rose's speculation that this is Dalton's baby. But I found the doctor's nurse in a nursing home in Fort Worth and she remembers Jenny giving birth."

Maddie's spirits fell. She might not have a sister, after all.

Dev hugged her again. "Hey, chin up. I'm not through looking. And I think Rose was right. When I asked around, everyone was very clear on the fact that Jenny was never seen with anyone but Dalton. They had made it very clear that they would marry, and people still remember them together even when Jenny was as young as fourteen. We'll only be sure after testing, but I doubt we'll find that this baby girl had any other father than Dalton Wheeler."

"But what if you can't find her?" Maddie brushed at the tears flooding her eyes.

"Hey," Dev squeezed her shoulders. "I'll find her. I'm as good at finding people as you are at preparing world-class meals."

Maddie heard the comforting smile in his voice

and lifted her head. "Please, Dev. It would mean the world to me."

He set her away from him, holding one shoulder and reaching into his pocket for a handkerchief. "Here—I can't send you back to Boone with red eyes."

Boone. Maddie's shoulders sagged. "I still don't have enough to tell him, do I?"

Dev shrugged. "That's your call."

"I'm so tired of sneaking around. But I don't know what else to do. Until we know she's alive—"

Dev nodded. "It could all be for nothing."

Maddie drew a deep breath. "Then I don't have any choice. He's had so much thrown at him. I'll just have to keep this a secret until you're certain."

"You're a lousy liar, Maddie. What if he shows up today?"

"Then I'll just have to make myself scarce. It won't be that much different. We've been tiptoeing around each other for almost two weeks now."

"Sam made a hell of a mess, didn't he?" Dev's eyes held sympathy.

Maddie glanced up. "I don't know whether to be glad or upset with him anymore. If he hadn't done what he did, I would never have known about any of this—my father, my grandmother, a sister…the house."

"Or Boone," Dev reminded her. His eyes held a knowing glint. "Are you sure you can go back to New York now?"

Maddie met his gaze in shock. "It's always been understood that I would."

He shrugged. "Things change."

"What does that mean?"

"Come on, Maddie. Don't try to tell me you haven't thought about staying. I've watched you when you talk about the house." His gaze bored into her. "And when you talk about Boone."

Maddie flushed. "There's nothing to decide. Boone might be attracted to me, but it's just physical. He can't wait for me to leave."

"Are you so sure about that?"

"Why? Has he said something to you?"

Dev laughed out loud. "Boone would just as soon punch me as talk to me more than necessary."

"I should have asked, though maybe it's none of my business. Are you having any luck finding Mitch?"

"I'm waiting for some information from Colorado, but nothing firm yet."

"Is it hard to juggle both searches? If so, mine can wait. Boone needs to find Mitch worse."

Dev shook his head. "You are some kind of woman, Maddie. I wonder if Boone has any idea how protective you are of him."

"He wouldn't like it. But I feel so badly for him. He's had such a lot of bad breaks."

"You haven't exactly had a great string of luck yourself."

"Oh, well." She straightened. "In just over two weeks, I'll be back in New York, fighting with tem-

peramental waiters and staving off my sous-chefs.''
For the first time in years, the prospect didn't sound
exciting.

Dev gave her a quick hug. ''I'll do my best to
find her before then, but if not, I'm always up for a
trip to New York.'' His gaze grew solemn. ''I'll find
her, Maddie. No matter what it takes. You just hang
in there.''

''Thanks, Dev.'' Grasping his shoulder, she rose
to her toes and kissed Dev's cheek.

Gripped by the emotion of the moment, neither
one noticed Boone passing by.

## *Chapter Ten*

He'd known better.

Boone jammed the trailer bolt shut with a clang. With long strides, he headed toward the cab of his truck.

"You gonna tell me what's eatin' you?" Jim asked.

"Nothing." He jerked the door open and slid inside. "I'll park this and be back to help you move the cattle."

Jim frowned but didn't argue.

Good thing, too. Boone didn't trust himself too much right now. Seeing Maddie in Marlowe's arms was something he guessed he should have been prepared for, but it had hit him hard.

It wasn't like the signs hadn't been there, like he

hadn't seen how well the two of them got on together. And it wasn't like he hadn't known all along that he and Maddie weren't suited, but—

But nothing. He'd been a fool to think that he had a chance. He'd let Maddie's smile blind him, let her laughter give him hope. And in a weak moment while he'd been gone, he'd actually tried to figure out a way to help her buy The Dinner Bell. That's how desperate he'd gotten to find a reason to keep her here.

Despite what he'd seen between her and Marlowe before today, he'd even given thought to asking her out on a real date. A mirthless grin twisted his lips. Seeing her in Marlowe's arms had put paid to that idea.

*Damn you, Sam.* The next two weeks looked endless. He had new stock; he couldn't just up and leave, no matter how painful it would be to have Maddie there and know that she preferred another man.

Boone leapt out of his truck and unhitched the trailer beside the barn. Then, there where no one could see, he slammed his fist into the wall. The pain in his hand couldn't hold a candle to the pain in his heart.

For Boone realized that he'd gone and done exactly what he'd sworn never to do.

He'd fallen in love, and fallen hard. For a woman he could never have.

*Gallagher men love only once.* And he'd done it with the wrong woman.

He wondered if Sam was watching him now.

If so, he must be laughing.

It was already dark when Maddie returned from driving the country roads for hours. When she saw Boone's truck parked at the house, her heart gave a little leap—then a twist of nerves.

No lights were on in the house. Maybe he was so tired he'd already gone to bed. She hoped so; she wasn't looking forward to keeping her feelings under wraps.

She was exhausted after running the gamut of emotions: thrilled that she might have a sister, afraid that Dev might never find her sibling or that when he did, she would want nothing to do with Maddie— or worse, that something bad had happened to her.

Then there were her worries over Boone's reaction when he found out. On top of that was the longing to see him, and beyond that, the qualms about whether or not she wanted him to have missed her.

Her head awhirl with too many thoughts, Maddie almost fell over the pile at the back door before she could hit the light switch in the kitchen.

"Don't turn it on." Boone's voice, deadly calm.

"What's wrong? What is all this?"

"It's my stuff. I'm clearing it out. Go ahead and move Marlowe in here. It's your house, but I don't have to stay and watch it."

Maddie couldn't process the words. "What? Why would I move Dev in here?"

"Don't play innocent, Maddie. I know about you and him. I saw you in town today, in the park."

Oh, no. What did he think he'd seen? "It's not what you think."

Boone's harsh laugh grated on her ears. "I've been there before. Oh, I never had to see my wife in the other man's arms, but I know when a woman is pining after a man who's somewhere else."

"Pining?" He thought she wanted Devlin? "Oh, my word. You think—" What could she do? How did she explain, without telling Boone what was going on?

"I don't have to think. I saw."

She heard the chair creak when he rose. She gazed at his outline in the moonlight spilling through the window.

"Did you follow me?"

"Yes."

"Why?"

"Like a fool, I was worried about you. I saw you take off, just as I was driving up toward the cutoff. You were in such a hurry, I thought something was wrong."

Maddie started toward him and banged her toe on a chair. "You don't have to leave."

"I should have moved out to the barn the first day. It would have been easier all the way around."

She wanted to throw something at him. "Just like that? You'd convict me without even asking what I was doing with Dev." In defiance, she flipped on the light.

Both of them blinked against the sudden glare.

"You've been sneaking around for a week, hanging up the phone when I walked into the room, whispering when I was nearby. All you had to do was ask me to leave. It's still your house."

"You think I'm the kind of woman who sneaks around?"

"It doesn't matter. We always knew it was temporary. You have every right to conduct an affair wherever you want."

His very certainty sent Maddie's temper shooting through the roof. She stepped over a pile of bedding and stalked across the floor, stabbing one finger at his chest. "You pompous oaf."

"What?" Boone's eyes widened in shock, then narrowed. "What the hell does that mean?"

"Oh, God." Maddie's laughter was a harsh bark in her chest. "I can't win." She paced the open portion of the floor.

"What are you saying?"

She whirled. "I can either tell you what I was doing and hurt you, or stay quiet and let you believe the worst of me."

Boone shrugged. "It's no skin off my nose if you want to have a fling with Devlin Marlowe."

Hurt wrestled with anger for dominance. Maddie stood there before him, her whole body shaking. "I am not having a 'fling,' as you call it, with Devlin Marlowe."

"Whatever you want to call it makes no difference to me. You're a free agent."

Maddie doubled up her fist and punched him square in the center of his chest. "Stop saying that, damn you. I'm not like that. I would never—" Maddie stopped short, stunned by the quick flash of pain in his eyes.

His jaw went tight and hard. "I won't stand by and be made a fool again, Maddie. You never lied to me that you would stay. Don't start lying now. You don't owe me anything. Just don't lie to me. That's all I ask."

She drew a deep breath. "All right. You want the truth? Just remember that I tried to protect you."

Boone frowned. "Protect me?"

"You'd better sit down, Boone. I honestly don't think you want to hear this."

"I'm fine right here." He crossed his arms over his chest. "And we already discussed whether or not you should be deciding what I'm ready to hear. Go on, Maddie."

She needed to occupy her hands, so she filled the tea kettle and started the burner beneath it.

"Come on. Stop stalling. I already know you care about Marlowe. Finish it."

"Dev is only helping me with research, no matter what you think you saw."

His jaw was tight. "What kind of research?"

"I found my grandmother's diary."

One eyebrow lifted, but he simply nodded for her to continue.

Maddie sucked in a deep breath and blew it out, praying for the right words. "Boone, my grandmother believed that your mother might have given birth to my father's child, and then given it up for adoption after my father vanished.''

If she'd hit him with a two-by-four, she doubted that he would have looked more shocked.

''What?'' But he was already shaking his head. ''No way. Never.''

''Boone, Dev has found out it's true. You have a sister, a half sister.''

''No. That's wrong. My mother would never—'' His voice turned arrow sharp. ''She loved children. She couldn't have any more after me, but she always wanted—''

When Maddie reached out to touch him, he jerked away.

''No—it's a lie. My mother would never have given away a child of hers. And she wouldn't have lied to us about it.''

Maddie had never seen him this agitated, not even on the night he rescued her from Hank. ''I'm sorry. I didn't want to tell you until I was sure, but—''

He whirled. ''Show me the proof.''

''Dev can't be sure yet that the baby was my father's, but no one ever saw Jenny with another man, so—''

''Stop—don't even think that she was some kind of tramp who—'' He headed for the door, then turned, hands clenched into fists, his shoulders tight bands of muscle. ''If any of this is true—I say *if*, mind you, then it's Dalton Wheeler's fault. He had no right to get her pregnant and then abandon her just like he abandoned everything else.''

Maddie knew that he spoke out of shock and hurt, but she had to defend the father she had loved. ''I doubt that he ever knew. But it doesn't matter. We have to find her.''

''Why are you doing this, Maddie? You're leaving. Why can't you leave the past alone?''

''I have to know. You can't keep me from finding her, Boone.''

''You were going to keep *me* in the dark.''

''Only until I knew for sure.''

Boone picked up his duffel bag and the pile of bedding and stepped toward the door. He jerked the door open and looked back.

''What other secrets do you plan to keep from me? What other decisions do you plan to make on my behalf? How much more will you tear up my life before you walk away?''

Maddie would have answered, if she'd had any idea what to say.

But she would have been talking to an empty room.

Boone punched down his pillow one more time and rolled over, looking for a spot that felt right. He'd brought a bedroll and sheets, so the hay wasn't the problem, he knew.

His problem was trapped inside his skin.

A sister. Half sister. His mother's child, with a man he'd grown up believing was a murderer.

*Maddie, why the hell couldn't you leave it alone?*

But he knew why. She had no family. She hadn't had the benefit of knowing where she belonged, as he had. Right or wrong, despite all the harm Sam had done after Boone's mother had died, Boone had grown up with a sense of place, had known his roots. He'd grown up with a grandfather who had taken him fishing and let him smoke his first—and only—cigarette. He'd known a sense of community. Maddie had been moved around all her life.

But thinking about his mother having a child with another man…it didn't go down easily. She had often said how much she wished for a daughter, but Boone and Mitch had taken it as teasing. All those years, had she longed for a child that she'd had to give up?

A sister. Boone thought of her as a baby, yet realized with a shock that she would be older than either him or Mitch. Would she have his mother's blond hair? His own blue eyes or the gray eyes that Maddie said she'd inherited from her father?

Would she want to be found? It would break Maddie's heart if she didn't—if she turned away. No matter how the news had rocked Boone's memories of his mother, or how much a part of him wished he'd never forced Maddie to answer, another part of him wanted to step in and protect her from this unknown woman's potential to hurt her.

It would devastate her if this sister denied the connection. For a moment, Boone remembered the look on Maddie's face when she told him that she had to know.

While part of Boone wanted all of this to go away, another part of him realized that he had cause to rejoice.

If this sister was real, he and Maddie would have a connection for as long as they lived. Not that she would welcome it, after the way he'd taken her news.

And he didn't want to think about a lifetime of crossing paths with Maddie and some other man. Or having to hear about Maddie bearing some other man's children.

But there wasn't another man yet. At that moment, Boone let himself feel the full impact of Maddie's insistence that there was nothing between her and Devlin Marlowe, and his spirits soared. She hadn't been having an affair behind his back. For a few seconds, he let himself feel a fierce spurt of hope.

Then he remembered how rough he'd been tonight. Maddie forgave easily, but where did her tolerance end?

And how could he claim forgiveness, yet again?

But Boone knew that he would try. Rising from his makeshift bed, he pulled on his boots, then realized that it was two o'clock in the morning. A little early to go begging, hat in hand.

Even if Maddie forgave easily again—not that he'd earned it—she deserved her rest.

There would be no sleep for him, however. Dancer snorted restlessly in her stall. Might as well go check on her, since he couldn't sleep, anyway.

At two in the morning, Maddie gave up on sleep and headed for the kitchen to get a glass of water.

Through the window she saw a light on in the barn. Maybe Boone couldn't sleep, either. Little wonder.

She'd handled it poorly. She'd known all along that the news of this sister would be a lot for Boone to swallow. What she hadn't realized was that the stories Vondell and Jim had withheld revolved around Boone's unfaithful wife.

Maddie had known that the woman named Helen had hated it here. But never once had anyone told her that she'd cheated on Boone. No wonder he'd been upset about the whispered phone calls, the times when she'd made excuses to drive into town.

She'd really botched it—the whole thing. Boone was right—she was making decisions for him as if he couldn't make his own. Sure, she'd had good intentions, but Maddie kept hearing his voice in her head.

*Why are you doing this? You're leaving.*

What right did she have, really, to dig up old secrets when they impacted him as much as her? He was right. She had no place here, but everything she did left a mark on him, too.

*I have to know.* And she did. If there was a chance that she had a sister out there somewhere, Maddie would go to the ends of the earth, looking for her.

But that didn't mean that she could continue to forge ahead without talking to Boone. She owed him an apology. Maybe now was as good a time as any. If that light in the barn didn't mean he was awake, she'd turn right around and come back.

But maybe, just maybe, she could settle things down and let each of them get some sleep.

So Maddie ran upstairs and threw on jeans and a shirt, not even bothering with underwear or socks. Then she ran to the barn, grateful for the moonlight that paved her way.

When she walked inside, she heard his voice, talking soft and low. She headed in that direction, stopping only long enough to pat Fancy's head. Fancy nickered to her, and at the noise, Boone stepped out in the aisle.

"Hi," Maddie said, throat tight.

"Hi," Boone answered. "Can't sleep?"

She shook her head. "You?"

He gestured with a nod toward the stall. "Full moon tonight. I'm betting Dancer goes into labor."

Silence. Maddie dug one toe in the dirt and spoke. "I'm sorry I did a bad job of delivering the news. I never wanted to hurt you. I know how you feel about your mother."

Boone shrugged and walked closer. "There's no easy way to say something like that. I didn't handle it well. I just—I don't know how to feel about that. The woman I knew wanted a dozen children."

"In those days, she was bound to feel that she had no choice. If you weren't married, you gave your child up or had a backstreet abortion. I can't imagine your mother doing that.''

Boone shook his head. ''No, she would never end a child's life.'' He stared hard at Maddie. ''And it wasn't fair for me to blame your father. You're probably right. Maybe he never knew.''

''My grandmother's diary said Jenny left town for seven months before she came back and married your father a few months later.''

''Just long enough.'' Boone shook his head. ''I can't imagine that my father ever knew.''

''Do you remember the part of his letter that said that there was always a sadness in Jenny?''

Boone nodded.

''Maybe it wasn't losing my father, like Sam always thought. Maybe it was the baby.''

She saw a shadow cross his face. ''What is it?''

''Nothing.'' He shook his head, then suddenly he stopped. ''No. That's not true. I accused you of holding back secrets, but I've held back my own.''

Maddie felt like holding her breath for fear he'd change his mind and clam up. ''You have a right to your secrets. We all do.''

Boone stared at her hard and for a long moment, then seemed to make up his mind. ''My wife was pregnant when she died with her lover in a sailing accident. She never even told me about the baby. I didn't learn about it until she was gone, when her mother announced it to me after the funeral.'' The shadow fell across his rugged features again. ''I don't know why it hits me so hard. I never knew that child, never held it in my hands. But it still hurts.'' He looked up. ''How much harder did it hit my mother to bear a child and have to give it up?''

''I'm so sorry, Boone,'' Maddie barely whispered. ''You would have been a wonderful father.''

Boone's look was grateful. ''I've done a lot of things wrong in my life, but I sure would have tried.''

Tears welled in Maddie's eyes, tears for children lost and children unborn, for this son who had lost his father the day his mother died. Tears for a missing brother, a lost sister. So many tears needed, and so little she could do.

And then Boone's arms surrounded her and held her close. Maddie nestled into his embrace and knew a moment of such piercing longing that she could barely breathe.

No words passed between them, but words weren't needed. Too often, words had driven them apart.

Maddie slid her arms around Boone's wide chest and clung tightly. Then the need for comfort melted like candle wax under the heat of a desire too long denied.

She lifted her head and saw her yearning mirrored in his eyes. ''Boone, please...'' She didn't have the words to tell him what she wanted, to tell him that she didn't want him to be noble—not this time.

*Ah, Maddie,* Boone thought. *Such sweetness. Such a generous heart.* He wanted, just for a moment, to stop fighting what must be and take shelter in Maddie's bright glow. "Oh, God, Maddie, I don't want to fight this any longer."

"Then don't," Maddie whispered.

His caution burned to cinders. Boone lowered his mouth to hers and heard her quick inhalation of surprise.

Then they were there in the landscape of their dreams—the forbidden territory they'd skirted for long days and endless nights. Everything that separated them faded, crushed by the urgent need of one heart for another.

When Boone's lips touched hers, Maddie felt the spark through every cell in her body. Her eager hands joined her eager heart, and she welcomed Boone to all she had, all she was.

Boone thought his own heart would burst as he slid his tongue inside Maddie's mouth and felt her fingers grip his back and bring them closer. Along every inch of the front of his body, Maddie's curves fit him like a second skin.

His body leapt in answer. Boone wanted nothing more than to drive into Maddie's sweet flesh and lose himself. Grasping for control, he sank one hand into her hair and turned her deeper into his kiss. With the other hand, he gripped the tender curve of her hip. When Maddie moaned, he broke the kiss, sliding his tongue down the long, slender column of her neck. He wanted to brand her, to mark her with his mouth on every inch of her skin. At the tender juncture where her pale throat met her shoulder, Boone used his mouth to seal Maddie as his.

Boone couldn't stop to think, to reason out how or why he would make it so. He simply...wanted.

Maddie thrilled at the passion of Boone's strong grip, his fierce possession. He rocked against her, and she met his hunger, measure for measure.

Boone growled low in his throat, and Maddie smiled. She wanted him crazy, too crazy to think, too far gone to be honorable.

They were past the time for noble sacrifices, past the time for reason. Now was the time for the heart to meet the body, for flesh to seal flesh in naked, greedy hunger. Maddie wanted her hands on Boone, on his naked skin, on the body she'd dreamed of, night after lonely night. With a small cry, she pulled away to tear at his shirt.

Boone tensed to jerk her back until he saw what she wanted. Then with a marauder's smile, he left just enough distance for her hands, one hand gripping her hair to anchor her mouth to his.

And with that mouth, he drove her insane. Maddie's fingers fumbled on buttons that she could not see, while Boone did wicked things to her with lips and teeth and tongue.

Finally, Maddie got his shirt open. She sacrificed a button or two, but she had to touch him—now. Both hands spread wide, she laid her palms on the burning skin of his chest.

Boone sucked in a gasp; his nostrils pinched. He glanced down at her pale hands spread across his golden skin.

And then he smiled, slow and wicked. "My turn."

Maddie licked her lips and flexed her fingers, scraping her nails lightly across his flesh.

Boone inhaled sharply, but kept his eyes on the buttons of her shirt, his large fingers clumsy in their haste. Under his breath, he muttered dark imprecations.

Maddie leaned forward and licked a slow stroke across his chest, just above one nipple.

With firm hands on her shoulders, Boone pushed her back so he could finish undoing her shirt. "I said, my turn." And then he smiled—a smile that Maddie had never before seen. A smile so full of seductive promise that all the air vanished from Maddie's lungs.

Then she laughed that sultry chuckle that had never failed to hit Boone right in his gut. Her smile dared him to push the edge, to test the borders. Maddie was so valiant with her heart, so unafraid of her passion.

And he was so hard that he hurt.

But he was not going to rush this, no matter how his body screamed for release, no matter how his insides had turned to pure fire at her touch.

That mouth of hers—that sassy, sexy mouth. If he lived to be a hundred, he would never get enough of Maddie's mouth.

With one last jerk, without apology he sent her buttons flying. "Too many damn buttons," he muttered.

And then fell silent.

"No bra?" he croaked.

Maddie's smile could make a man weep. "No panties, either."

Boone closed his eyes and implored the heavens.

Then Maddie laughed, and Boone was done with patience.

He swept her up in his arms and bore her away to his makeshift bed. "Say 'no' now if you mean it, Maddie. I've waited for you too long."

Maddie drew a zipper motion across her lips, then grasped his head in her hands and kissed him with a fervor that sent flames shooting down his nerve paths.

"You and that damn sexy mouth," he muttered. Then his mouth came down on hers.

When he laid her on the sheets still scented from his body, the hay perfuming the air around them, Maddie thought there could be no more perfect place. The bedroll provided protection from stray stalks of hay, and they were far away from the house and all its memories of sorrow.

Then Maddie thought no more, as she caught her first full view of Boone's naked chest. The muscles of a working man stood out in relief, lightly covered with golden hair slightly darker than that on his head. His belly was flat and firm, his waist and hips narrow. Her gaze traveled down the fine line of hair on his belly, then farther downward to blatant evidence of Boone's desire for her.

Never before had anyone wanted her this badly.

Never before had anyone brought such raw, naked power to the act of love.

Boone's fingers unsnapped her jeans with one flick, then drew her zipper down slowly. He bent over and trailed his tongue down her neck, flicking it lightly over the shadowed valley, then one smooth slide around the curve of her breast, just missing her nipple.

Maddie arched toward him, her body pleading to feel him suckle her. All along her body, Maddie wanted him to touch her—every inch. Urgent fingers gripped his shoulders as he hovered above her breast, waiting.

Then Boone moved away, and Maddie wanted to scream.

Until she felt his tongue inside her zipper. Inch by inch, he lowered the metal tab carefully, sliding one finger beneath to guard tender flesh. When he finished unzipping, he didn't remove her jeans immediately. Instead, he parted them slightly and licked one slow glide down the *V*.

Maddie couldn't breathe. His tongue stopped scant inches away from her aching center. His breath warm on her belly, he swirled one slow, maddening circle through fine tendrils of hair.

Maddie dug her fingernails into his back and arched against him.

And Boone chuckled.

''Boone,'' she moaned. ''Now.''

''Not yet, sweetheart. You're killing me, but I'm not going to rush this.'' He rose above her.

So Maddie took her own revenge, drawing from her imagination to extract a toll from him as well. Gripping her fingers in his hair, she laid her mouth on his and swirled her tongue inside the dark heat of his mouth.

Boone took the kiss deeper, wrenching a moan from deep inside her chest. He wrapped iron-hard arms around her and took her diving with him into bliss.

Maddie slid her hand inside his waistband, his impressive hardness easy to reach. Boone jerked at her touch, and Maddie smiled against his mouth.

"God, Maddie. I want you so badly."

"Now, Boone," she pleaded. "I need you now."

In seconds, he had them both naked.

And there he was, standing above her, a golden man whose body wore the scars of a life lived by his wits. Maddie lifted her arms in welcome.

For just one moment, Boone stayed where he was and drank in the sight of her—long dark hair tumbled across the sheets of the bed where he'd been tossing only minutes before.

She was so perfect for him: the slender shoulders that bore life's burdens with such cheer; the lush, full breasts more than enough to fill his hands; the narrow waist curving out to form a woman's hips, descending into legs long enough to make a grown man cry.

But what struck Boone like a fist in the chest was more than Maddie's physical beauty, more than any curve of breast or hip or thigh. In the act of love, as in all of Maddie's life, it was her generous spirit that made Maddie shine.

Lying on his makeshift bed, Maddie could have been the Queen of Sheba...Cleopatra...Delilah. Pouring out from Maddie's tempting body was the beauty of Maddie's soul. A man would gladly die for this woman. The darkened hollows of Boone's heart cried out in longing.

He wanted her as he'd wanted no other before her, though he did not kid himself that they would ever have another night.

But if this night was all they had, he would make it one Maddie would never forget.

Arms open, Maddie watched sorrow sweep over Boone's face. She wanted to scare away sorrow, to replace it with joy, to give Boone all that he deserved.

Such a noble man, filled with valor and strength and determination. Life had not been easy on Boone, but Boone was far harder on himself. Maddie wanted to kiss away his sorrow, put a final seal on his pain. How could any woman not cherish this man?

Helen had been a fool. Inside this man lay all the treasure any woman would need. Maddie wished with her soul that she could make Boone understand. He blamed himself, and he'd been wrong.

All of a sudden, Maddie knew that losing Boone would steal a piece of her soul. Fear sent a shaft through her heart—for the pain to come.

But Boone would not let her stay frozen. The formidable strength of his will, the raw power of the man, conquered her fright.

Soon, his hands banished doubt, drove away fear. Maddie blossomed under his caress, feeling every nerve spring to life.

He was everywhere, touching everything, refusing to be denied. His tongue slicked her body, his hands cupped her breasts, his hardness slipped between her thighs, and Maddie wanted no escape.

Power. Madness. Desire beyond measure.

Maddie felt his hot breath on her skin, felt the moist kiss of his tongue.

With every touch, every sigh, Maddie gave up the deepest part of herself to this man—a man like no other.

Boone parted Maddie's thighs and heard her quick hiss.

He suckled her breasts and heard her moan.

With every stroke of her body, he lost himself in the magic that was Maddie Rose.

Her eyes went black with desire, spark-shot with longing.

His body screamed for release, yet he could not bear for this to end.

"Maddie," he gasped. *I love you.*

But the words stayed inside him, too new and too tender. Maddie had borne enough. He would not burden her further.

So he watched her eyes seek him out, heard the hitch in her breath. Then, when he could bear to be apart from her no longer—

He made her his own.

Maddie cried out at the feel of him—at last inside her, where he belonged.

Boone heard her gasp as he touched the deepest part of her. Maddie's sweet flesh surrounded him, gloved him like softest velvet. In all his life, he had never felt the sense of belonging that he felt right now.

*Hold me tight, Maddie.*

And she did, wrapping the long legs of his dreams around his waist and pulling him even deeper.

"Hold on, Maddie girl," Boone murmured. "I can't wait much longer. I've wanted you too long."

"Oh, Boone…" Maddie dug her fingers into his hair and arched against him, pressing heated kisses against his neck. "Don't wait…please don't wait."

Boone withdrew, and Maddie whimpered.

Another long stroke…another taste of heaven.

Soon there was no thought, no reason, nothing but the rush of blood, the press of flesh, the slick heat of body against body, denied too long.

Maddie felt her mind leave her, felt the moment when all she was belonged to Boone. With clever fingers and dangerous tongue, he drove past her reason and made her burn.

"Boone," she whimpered, feeling herself in a new sphere, a place she'd never been.

"Come, Maddie. Come with me," he whispered.

And so she did.

"Look at me," he demanded. "I want you to know it's me who's inside you."

Maddie's eyes had drifted shut, but flew open again at Boone's command.

Blue eyes could burn with fire, she discovered. Could slice through her, laser-hot.

"I want—" She didn't know what she wanted, except him.

"I know," Boone answered. "Come with me. Make the heavens burn."

With every stroke, Maddie flew higher, losing herself in the wonder of this man. Boone filled her, completed her…made her want to crawl inside his fire and burn to cinders.

Boone drove her higher, watching Maddie's face and feeling her body squeeze tightly around him. He wanted it to last forever. He wanted to fly with her now.

And then it was too late for either of them. The fire, so long denied, would be denied no longer.

Boone took Maddie's mouth as though it were the last sustenance he'd ever know.

Maddie opened wider, urged him deeper, beyond the limits of her body.

And they flew, on wings of eagles, beyond any dimension either had ever known. The power of the moment stunned them speechless, sent them soaring.

For one precious moment, Boone and Maddie became one. One heart. One mind. One soul.

When he could think again, Boone rolled to his back while holding her tightly, unwilling to break their connection. Maddie lay boneless against him, her breath warm against his throat as he stroked her hair with one hand. Hearing her soft, catchy sighs of contentment as she lay in his arms, Boone knew that this was all of heaven he would ever need.

*I love you, Maddie,* he wanted to say.

And he almost did. But something within him hesitated.

And then it was too late. Fate conspired with reality to force a different spin.

Dancer cried out in pain.

And the only future Boone could imagine crashed courses with the one that his wounded soul craved.

## Chapter Eleven

Three hours later, a faint light pearled the sky. Inside the barn, no one noticed.

Boone stole a look at Maddie and saw dark hollows beneath her eyes. More than once, he'd urged her to go to the house and seek her bed.

But not once had Maddie faltered. Even now, at the end of a long night with no sleep and too much emotion, she held steady on her course. Her shirt was buttoned crooked, the last three buttons missing. Maddie hadn't turned a hair, had simply tucked it into her jeans and gone on.

Damn. What lousy timing. All his attention had to stay on the mare and the unborn foal that would be his future. Never mind that it was a future that no longer seemed enough.

He wanted Maddie. It was that simple. Not logical, not practical, not possible—but he still wanted her. In his bed, yes, but also in his life.

For a few tempting seconds, Boone considered asking. Then he looked at Maddie—really looked—and realized his folly.

She looked like a Madonna, albeit one with straw in her hair. Dirt smudged her face and filled her fingernails. She had never seemed more beautiful to him. But was it fair to ask her to live like this, when she could have so much more?

Dancer strained, and Maddie soothed, singing to her in a low, soft voice. It had been this way since he and Maddie had scrambled into their clothes, not even granted enough time to linger in the afterglow of the most explosive lovemaking of his life.

Dancer's belly hardened like oak. The contraction rippled through her, and the inexperienced mare grunted low. Yet again, she picked up her head as though trying to understand what was happening.

Maddie never stopped crooning and stroking. "It's all right, sweetie. They're brutes, all of them. Stay away from the male animal. It's my best advice."

Then she looked up at Boone and winked.

Damn, she was magnificent.

"I feel like I should be defending my sex," he said.

"Don't waste your breath. We're not listening, are we, girl?" But her eyes twinkled with mischief.

He wanted to ask, but now was not the time. *Was it as incredible for you? Did you feel what I felt?*

Boone couldn't believe himself. He'd always cared about his partner's satisfaction, true, but never had he needed to know that he had been the best. He never left a woman wanting, but now that wasn't enough. He wanted to send Maddie to the stratosphere, to be the one she couldn't forget.

To be the one and only.

To be the last.

*You're losing it, Boone. You know that won't happen. Be grateful that you had last night.*

Then the mare's eyes widened in panic, and there was no more time to think.

Maddie looked at him, worry in her eyes, but still she stayed calm. "Getting close?"

Boone smiled grimly. "Very close. You can leave if you want."

Maddie shook her head and blew a strand of hair out of her eyes, never taking her hands off the horse. "Not on your life. We're a team, aren't we, girl?"

A hell of a woman. Maddie might have spent her life in cities, but she was no city girl. He should have seen it sooner.

Boone bent his head and concentrated on the task at hand.

How she wished she knew what he was thinking. Maddie schooled herself to pay attention to the mare and not dream about Boone, but it wasn't easy. Her mind kept drifting back, wanting to remember his kiss, his touch…his powerful body filling her and sending her soaring.

It had never been like that for her, ever. Maddie watched Boone's hands on the mare and remembered a day in the garden when she had thought she understood how those hands would feel on her.

She had understood less than nothing.

For as long as she lived, Maddie would never forget this night. But one night would not be enough.

What did Boone think? Had it meant anything to him beyond a meeting of bodies?

She was doing it again: measuring herself by someone else. *You have to be enough for yourself, Maddie. No one else can do it.* The words sounded so simple, so logical when her father had drilled them into her head. But now Maddie wondered.

Had he told her that because of all he'd lost? Had it been his way to overcome all that was missing? If he had loved Jenny half as much as Maddie—

Loved Boone?

No. She couldn't. Shouldn't.

But it didn't matter what was sensible. She did.

"Okay, Maddie. You ready? It's showtime."

Boone's voice scattered Maddie's thoughts like leaves in a windstorm.

"What do I do?"

He glanced up, his concentration fierce, but his voice was gentle when he answered. "You're doing fine just like you are. She's new at this, and she needs someone to tell her she's all right."

"Will she be? All right, I mean?"

One more quick glance. One fleeting smile. "I think so."

Maddie saw the lines of strain on his face. He'd mentioned before his concerns about the mare, his hopes for the foal. Maddie left him alone and turned her concentration on the mother. "That's a good girl," she cooed, stroking the mare's head slowly. "I know it hurts, but soon you'll have your baby and you'll say it's worth it."

"I thought you said all men were pigs, or something like it." Amusement threaded through the strain in Boone's voice.

"This is just between us girls. You're not supposed to be listening."

Dancer picked up her head again, and Maddie thought she saw fear in the mare's eyes. Once more, she murmured and stroked the fine, proud head.

"Almost there," Boone said. "Easy, girl. Let her go now, Maddie, and get ready to move back. She'll probably try to get up as soon as it's out. If you want to come around and watch, just be sure you stay back."

Maddie stroked the mare one more time, then stepped away and stared. Two thin legs protruded, guided by Boone's hands. Then she heard a sound that she could only describe as "squishy," and the foal slid out into Boone's waiting arms.

All wet, dark hair, mucus and membrane and blood, the baby still seemed a miracle to Maddie. Boone busied himself cleaning mucus from the foal's nose and mouth. "Would you hand me that towel behind you, please?"

When Maddie handed it to him, Boone looked up at her with triumph in his eyes, and Maddie's heart gave a hard thump.

"May I touch her? Him?"

"Him. It's a colt." Boone stared at her across the stall, and in the glow of his eyes, Maddie found herself unable to move.

"In a minute you can. Just don't get in the mare's way. She needs to smell him and let him smell her. That way they will bond." Boone gently laid the colt down in the straw and drew Maddie over to his side. Maddie knelt beside him, overcome with awe.

"He's beautiful, Boone. It's incredible. I've never seen anything so wonderful."

Boone met her smile with his own. Silently, they watched the mare clean her baby.

Maddie threw her arms around Boone and hugged him hard. "Thank you for this. I'll never forget it."

Boone started to protest that he was filthy, but it was already too late. When Maddie pulled away, she was filthy, too.

But she didn't seem to notice; her eyes shone, her smile was wide. "It's a miracle, isn't it? Do you ever get tired of seeing it?"

"Never," he replied, but he could have been talking about watching her. How had he ever thought her wrong for this place? How had he lived so long without her joy?

Dancer had sniffed and licked the colt from head to tail. It was time for Boone to get to work.

He talked while he took care of the umbilical cord, then began handling the colt, explaining to Maddie what he was doing. "I'm getting him used to being touched right from the start. It will make him easier to train if he bonds with me as much as with his mother."

He took the colt through a routine that they would repeat for days to come, manipulating his legs and feet, touching every part of his body, not letting the colt rise until he finished.

"I'm teaching him that I'm the head horse, that he is to follow me in whatever I say. That's why I didn't let him get up right away. Now I will. His legs will be wobbly."

Boone rose and came to stand beside Maddie, while the colt struggled to its feet.

Maddie couldn't help but smile. "I can't believe he can stand so soon." Then she giggled as the colt staggered like a two-day drunk. She turned to Boone. "We can't prop him up?"

"You'll be amazed at how steady he'll be even by tonight." Pride filled Boone's voice, but Maddie heard the exhaustion beneath.

That, she could do something about. "I'm going to fix us some breakfast."

"You don't have—"

"Boone. Don't even say it."

His look was sheepish. "I'd crawl over broken glass for a cup of coffee."

"A simple thank you will do." Maddie smiled.

"Thank you." Boone smiled back. He opened his mouth as if he wanted to say something else. Then he shook his head.

"What?"

"I owe you an apology. You may be a city girl, but you handled yourself like a pro."

Maddie wasn't sure that she'd ever heard a sweeter compliment. "I won't say I told you so," she teased. Then she sobered. "Thank you for letting me stay. It was incredible."

"You were pretty incredible yourself." In Boone's eyes shone another memory of the night.

Maddie wanted to linger, but Boone was hungry and tired, she knew. If she didn't leave now, she never would. "I—I'd better go."

His voice turned neutral. "I'll come as soon as I'm sure everything's okay here. Jim will be in soon, and he can watch them."

Maddie wanted to say something, to talk about last night. But Boone had already turned back to mother and baby.

He had work to do. There would be time later.

Maddie emerged from the bathroom, her hair still wet, but all of her much cleaner. She already had coffee perking. She'd take a cup to Boone before she started breakfast.

She was halfway down the stairs when the phone rang. Maddie glanced at the clock. Who would be calling at seven in the morning?

"Hello?"

"Darling, I'm so glad I reached you. Is it too early?"

Régine. Even on eastern time, it was early for someone whose restaurant closed well after midnight.

"Not as early for me as it is for you, I'll bet."

The older woman's laugh sounded rusty. "I wouldn't be up at this godforsaken hour if it weren't important."

"Is something wrong?"

"Maddie, things have changed here. I can't wait two more weeks for you."

"Oh. I understand. You have plenty of prospects, I'm sure."

"That's not what I mean. I want you, Maddie. Only you. I'm convinced, more than ever, that you are our destiny."

Régine had always had a flair for the dramatic.

"I can't leave here, not yet."

"I'm prepared to up the ante." Then her voice turned tentative in a way Maddie had never heard this hard-edged woman speak. "Maddie, my doctor has discovered a lump in my breast. He says it's manageable, but I have to go into the hospital. I may be there for a while. I need you here."

"Oh, Régine, I'm so sorry."

"Spare me the pity." The other woman's voice was dry. "Just help me out. I'm prepared to offer you an ownership stake in the restaurant now."

"Ownership?" In a place far beyond anything

Maddie could expect to own? But she couldn't leave yet—Boone would lose this house. "Régine, I—Anthony can run things for you." Her maître d' had been with her for years and knew everything Régine knew.

"It's what you want, isn't it? To own your own restaurant?"

"Yes, I've always wanted to own my own place. And Sancerre is everything I've ever dreamed, but—"

"I'm not going to let you tell me no, Maddie. You've lost your perspective. You can't seriously think to give this up for some dusty cowboy. You don't belong there. You could be the toast of the town here."

"I—I promised Boone I would stay."

"Maddie, I need you. That place is just a house. You said he would still have plenty of land, even without the house. And he can probably buy the house from those other people. You won't need the money from him if you come in with me. Let him have the place, if it makes you feel better, but don't be foolish, Maddie. This is your future."

New York had never seemed farther away. But Régine had been her friend for a long time. She had even helped Maddie extract herself from the Robert fiasco.

But Maddie had promised Boone she'd stay.

"Don't answer me now. Tell me you'll call back tonight. Think about it, Maddie. Think hard. You've worked for years for this. And I need you."

Maddie could resist anything else, but a plea from her cynical friend was like water in the desert. Régine never pleaded.

"I'll call you tonight, Régine."

"I'll be waiting."

Maddie hung up the phone with a sinking heart.

"You have to go." Boone's voice startled her.

Maddie whirled. "What?"

"You can't throw away a golden opportunity. I remember what you said. That place is at the top of the heap, and she's giving you ownership—didn't I hear that right?"

Maddie nodded dully.

"It's what you said you wanted. You're good, and this is your chance."

"But the Caswells—"

"Leave the Caswells to me. You can't blow this chance, Maddie. It's exactly what you've always wanted."

"Yes, but—" She'd thought so. But after last night…

"Then the answer is simple." His voice was clear and brisk as he walked to the coffeepot and poured himself a cup. "You have to go." He turned away from her. "Do I have time for a quick shower?"

Maddie didn't know what to think, what to say. So she busied herself with breakfast. "Will twenty minutes be enough?"

"That will be fine." He started from the room.

"Boone—" She wanted to stop him, to—what? Beg him to let her stay? If he wanted that, he would have asked her. Boone wasn't shy about speaking his mind.

"What?" He didn't turn.

Maddie drew in a deep breath. "Two eggs or three?"

"Three." His voice never faltered.

When she heard his steps on the stairs, Maddie clutched the sink with white-knuckled fingers.

*I will not cry.* But Maddie had to blink hard to see her way to the stove.

Boone stood in the doorway to the bathroom and tried to remember why he was here.

*You should be an actor, after that performance.*

But what else could he do? It was within her grasp to have everything she'd dreamed. How could he make her stay for two more weeks and lose her chance?

*You want more than two weeks, and you know it. And the Caswells aren't going to bargain with you. Harold Caswell and Sam hated each other.*

It didn't matter. Boone had to do what was right for Maddie. He'd figure out something about the house later. God knew he'd have plenty of time to do nothing but think.

And to miss her. If only she had expressed any doubts about leaving... But he'd heard her on the phone. Her only argument was that she'd made a promise to him, not that she'd changed her mind.

Promises could be broken. There were other places on the ranch to build himself a house. He wasn't sure he could stay in this one, anyway, once Maddie was gone. If he'd thought it was haunted before... He would hear the echo of Maddie's laughter in every room. See her face in every corner.

Boone's shoulders sagged. How the hell was he going to stand being in this place without her?

Then he straightened. The least he could do was to make it as easy as possible for her to leave. Her strong sense of honor could keep her from jumping at the opportunity of a lifetime, if he didn't do this. Two weeks from now, she would still leave, but without that chance.

*You could ask her to stay.*

He could—but he wouldn't. If even once he'd heard her voice doubts about leaving... If he had any sense that she might—

No. He had no more to offer her now than the day she'd arrived. An unexciting life with a man who could seldom afford a vacation. A life of hard work and little profit. The nearest fine dining or music or museums hours away in Fort Worth or Dallas.

He had one more thing he could offer, but it wasn't much of a bargain. He had a worn-out heart that had never figured out how to manage love the right way.

All in all, not much to tempt a woman who could have the world at her feet.

No, he would do the right thing by Maddie.

If it killed him.

Magic didn't last. *Stop being a romantic, Maddie. Look at this for what it is.*

She'd said it before. Now she had to believe it.

The night had been magic, but the opportunity of a lifetime dangled before her. She had to take it seriously. She had worked very hard to get where she was, and she couldn't afford to blow this.

So why didn't owning a piece of Sancerre make her heart sing? Why did she keep thinking about owning The Dinner Bell?

Maddie knew why. The Dinner Bell was closer to Boone.

But Boone had made it clear that she should grab this chance. He'd sounded confident that he could work things out with the Caswells so he would not lose the house.

If last night had meant as much to him as to her, she couldn't tell it now. Maddie had stripped her pride bare too often with Robert. She couldn't beg Boone. It would mean giving up all the progress she'd made since she'd come here.

She was strong. She would get through this. She would ask Boone one more time, to be absolutely sure he wouldn't lose this place that he loved. If he gave her the slightest sense that the house was at risk, she would stay, no matter what. Maddie didn't go back on her word.

But if he were certain, she would call Régine back. She would make arrangements, and then she would pack.

She would get out of here before she fell to pieces.

And she would hope that Sancerre needed her a

lot—so much so that she could drown herself in work.

And forget a golden man who had broken her heart, just as she'd known he could.

Boone looked at his empty plate in surprise. He hadn't tasted a single bite of a meal that he was sure had been excellent.

A long, silent meal.

Maddie looked up as if to say something, then paused to take a sip of her juice.

*Tell me you don't want to leave, that New York isn't important.*

But she didn't. "Are you sure you can work something out with the Caswells?"

A lead weight settled in his chest. From some place deep inside him, he drew on long-buried reserves. "It was your family that killed a Caswell, Maddie, not mine." He hated the stricken look on her face, but he had to convince her. "They'll deal with me. Their son Junior and I played football together in high school."

Maddie chewed on that full lower lip that drove him crazy. For an instant, he could remember her taste, remember the velvet feel of that lip between his own.

Boone clenched his fist around his napkin.

"If you're sure—" she said. "I guess I'd better call Régine back." Rising, Maddie picked up both their plates. Her eyes were worried. "I probably should leave today. You'll be all right until Vondell gets back?''

*No. I'll never be all right if you're not here.*

''Maddie, I've told you—''

A faint smile crossed her lips. ''I know—you can take care of yourself.''

*But I need you, anyway. I can't take care of the hole inside my heart.*

He didn't say that, though. He rose and took their glasses from the table. Standing by her at the sink, he remembered a night when he'd thought he'd die of longing to taste her, to touch her.

Now he'd done both. And the pain raged like a wounded beast inside him.

''Well—'' he said. ''I'd better get back to the barn and check on the colt.''

As he turned, he caught one quick glance of Maddie's face. There were tears in her eyes.

With an aching heart, Boone clenched his fists and walked toward the door.

*I have nothing to offer her. Nothing like what she could have.* But with every step, his heart cried out louder, howling to be heard.

''What will you name him?''

Boone couldn't imagine what she was asking. He turned. ''Name who?''

Tears rolled freely down her cheeks.

*Don't do this to me, Maddie. I'm trying to let you go. I'm trying to do the right thing for you.*

''The colt.'' Maddie sniffed hard and drew her shoulders up straight.

Valiant. Strong. A heart as big as the sky. She was everything he'd ever wanted, everything he'd ever need.

The words came out before he could stop them. "Don't go, Maddie." His heart thundered so loudly that he could barely hear her reply.

"What?" Her eyes widened.

"I said, don't go. Please. Stay with me." He hurried on, unable to stop himself now. "I know I don't have anything to offer compared to New York. The sky is the limit for you there. But if you stay and marry me, I'll do everything in my power to see that you never regret it. I'll work hard and save money so I can take you to those places you like. I know Morning Star isn't much, but—"

"Yes."

"I promise I'll—" He stopped cold. "What? What did you say?"

Then there she was again, the Maddie he loved. That smile that made the world bright bloomed beneath her tears. Those eyes sparkled again.

Nothing could be very wrong when Maddie was smiling.

"I said yes. I want to stay. We don't have to get married, but—"

He was across the floor in an instant, hauling her into his arms. "Yes, we do," he demanded. "I want to know you're mine, for good."

But honor required that he be sure she understood. He pulled back slightly. "I didn't make Helen happy. Maybe you should think about this. Don't be impulsive.''

''I'm always impulsive, Boone,'' she teased. Then she sobered. ''Would you change me?''

''I don't want to change anything about you. I just want to love you.''

Maddie searched his gaze. ''You were going to send me away because you thought it was what I wanted, weren't you?''

''You should still want it. I can't give you New York.''

''Making decisions for me, Boone?''

He had the grace to blush.

''I don't want New York,'' she said. ''I want you.''

Boone's eyes turned very serious. ''I'll never love another woman but you, Maddie. Gallagher men—''

''Love only once,'' she chimed in. ''That's good. 'Cause I'm pretty handy with a knife.''

He smiled, but his eyes were still serious. ''I could come with you to New York. You could still have that dream.''

If Maddie doubted that he loved her, here was ample proof. ''You mean that, don't you?''

''Yes.''

Maddie sighed and laid her head against his chest. ''You really do love me.''

''What about you, Maddie?'' She'd never heard him sound uncertain before.

She lifted her head and placed one hand on his heart. ''I would never ask you to leave. I don't want to leave, either. I've never belonged anywhere before. I love you, and I love this place. Here—'' she pressed against his heart ''—this is where home is now.''

Boone's eyes held all the love in the world as he lowered his lips to hers.

''Welcome home, Maddie.''

*Epilogue*

Maddie rushed toward Sam's old office, which she now shared with Boone. Vondell had found her in the garden, telling her that Dev had returned and wanted to meet with them both before tomorrow's wedding festivities. Maddie chewed her lip, hoping for good news about Mitch or their missing sister. It would be the best wedding present possible.

Though they had intended to have only a small, private ceremony with a justice of the peace, once word got out, Morning Star had been intent upon something completely different. It was amazing what could be done in two weeks. Maddie had gone to New York for three days to assure herself that Régine and Sancerre would be fine. She'd been stunned to see all that had been accomplished in her absence.

It was Vondell's doing, Maddie was certain. But she couldn't really complain. The romantic inside her wanted the world to see her joy, wanted to marry Boone in a sentimental, old-fashioned ceremony like those of Maddie's girlhood dreams. She would wear her grandmother's gown, and Régine had sent a family heirloom sixpence for Maddie's shoe.

There would be no one there to be her family, but she'd found replacements. Jim had asked to be allowed to give her away, and Velda and Vondell had been clucking over her for days. For a moment, Maddie wondered if she wanted to ask Boone to postpone the wedding, depending on Dev's news.

Not really. Anyway, Boone was determined to marry her as soon as possible, and Boone Gallagher was not an easy man to stall.

But oh, he was an easy man to love.

"Penny for your thoughts," said the voice that made Maddie's heart thump. Boone grabbed her by the waist, waylaying her before she reached the office. He pulled her into the stairwell and proceeded to remind her forcefully of what lay in store tomorrow night.

The man sure could kiss.

Soon Maddie didn't care who was waiting—or why.

Boone ended the kiss with a sigh of regret. "I can't wait to make you mine again. Are you sure we have to wait another day?" His eyes held smoldering promise.

"I don't know," she sighed. "I'm having trouble remembering why I think it's important to wait."

Boone exhaled sorrowfully. "So I have to be noble, is that what you're telling me?"

Maddie struggled to grin, as desire ran like honey through her body. "You're so good at it."

"And you, heartless woman, are going to drive me crazy before I get my hands on you again."

"Boone? Maddie? Devlin is waiting, and I've still got to get Maddie in that dress one more time," Vondell called from the kitchen.

Boone frowned. Maddie smiled. Both of them sighed.

He straightened and tucked her hair behind one ear. "I messed up your hair."

"I don't care."

"I'm not going to live long enough to make love to you," he muttered. "I'm going to die before tomorrow night."

Maddie tucked her hand in the crook of his arm and ushered him toward the office, grinning. "Don't whine, Boone. It's not heroic."

"Never wanted to be a damn hero, anyway," he grumbled.

Maddie stopped and turned. "Too late. You're already mine."

Boone shook his head and smiled, opening the door. "After you, heartless wench."

"Why, thank you, sir," Maddie simpered.

Devlin glanced up at the sound of their laughter, but not before Boone saw his frown.

"What is it?" Boone asked. "Is Mitch—"

"No—nothing's wrong. I just wish I could give

you the wedding present I wanted and tell you I've found them both.''

''What have you found?'' Maddie spoke up.

Dev looked at Boone first. ''I'm close to finding Mitch. I've tracked down his whereabouts four months ago. He was in New Mexico.''

Boone's brow furrowed. ''You really think you're close?''

''Oh, yeah, no question. It won't be much longer.''

Boone nodded. Maddie could feel the tension in his frame ease.

She spoke up. ''What about Dalton and Jenny's daughter?''

Dev's shoulders sagged. ''Not as close as I'd like, but I've got some promising leads in Houston. I'll head back there right after the wedding.'' He squared a look at Boone. ''Thanks for inviting me. I'm sorry that it's not all the wedding present I'd hoped to give.''

Maddie gave him a quick hug. ''It's a wonderful present, Dev.''

Dev set her away from him carefully, shooting glances toward Boone. ''Uh, Maddie—''

Maddie grinned at Boone. ''Oh, Boone doesn't mind. He knows I'm crazy about him.''

Boone pulled her into his side. ''Boone does mind. Keep your hands off my woman, Marlowe.'' But his eyes sparkled, and he held out a hand. ''Thank you. It may not be all you wanted to deliver, but it's hopeful news.''

Dev shook his hand. ''So you think you might

even call me by my first name if I find your brother?''

"Since I know you don't have designs on Maddie, I'll do it now." Boone chuckled. "Thanks, Dev. We appreciate all you're doing."

Then Boone looked at Maddie, his eyes full of promise. "Now, if that's all—"

"Wait." Dev cleared his throat, his face growing somber. "There's something else."

Boone stiffened at his tone. "What's that?"

Dev reached into his briefcase and drew out an envelope. "I have something for you."

Boone recognized his name written in Sam's bold hand. "Why now?"

"I don't pretend to understand Sam's thinking. All I know is that he asked me to hold this until after Maddie had been here thirty days. Yesterday was the thirtieth day."

"I don't want it."

"Boone—" Maddie cautioned, placing one hand on his arm. "Maybe it will be something good."

He had his doubts, but as he looked into Maddie's eyes, he realized that it didn't matter anymore what Sam had done. His father had brought Maddie into his life, for whatever reason, and that had been the best thing the man had ever done. It might not be what Sam had intended, but Boone didn't want to imagine his life without Maddie. Still, he didn't want any more of Sam's surprises to hurt her. If the letter inside was bad, he just wouldn't let her read it.

"It doesn't really matter," he said. "You're here. I have to thank him for that."

Maddie's smile reached into his heart like a warm, calming hand.

His life was so rich, so full of promise, now that Maddie was by his side. He couldn't wait until tomorrow to tell the world that she belonged to him.

But his fingers still trembled a little as he sliced open the envelope. A single sheet lay inside.

Son—
By now, anything may have happened between you and Dalton's daughter. At worst, I've done the right thing and given her a chance to keep her family home. If that's the case, you're probably mad as hell at me, and I can't blame you.

I've done a lot that was wrong by you, Boone. You didn't deserve it. I've never told you how proud I am of the boy who held this place together. Or the man who came back, even though it cost him a wife.

I didn't like Helen. I won't pretend I did. I wanted you to have a woman like your mother—a woman you could love with everything in you. Helen was never that kind of woman. She wanted you to be someone else. That was damn stupid of her. You're a fine man, just the way you are.

I'm going to hope that my best-case scenario happened—that you and Maddie Rose hit it off. No one can predict what will happen when a man and woman meet, but I like what I hear about her from Devlin's research. And she comes from good stock. Rose Wheeler had a hard life, but she took what was dealt and never let it turn her hard. And Dalton...well, bad as I did him, Dalton was my best friend and a good man. Not many would sacrifice what he did. Both of them knew how to love people, and from what I can tell, Maddie Rose does, too.

You need that, Boone. You need someone to make you laugh. I hear she laughs easily, that she's got color and spark to her. I don't want you to live out your life alone.

But either way, I don't expect you to forgive me. I missed a lot of years with you and your brother. I'll never forgive myself for that. I just couldn't get past losing Jenny—but she wouldn't be proud of what I did.

I should have sent for you sooner. Now the doc says there's no time. Just as well, I guess. I don't know how I'd face you. I just hope to God you can find Mitch and bring him home. And I'm going to hope, like some sentimental old fool, that Maddie Rose is there when you do. Dalton and Rose would be happy.

I don't know if it's much solace to know I paid for my mistakes. I lost two fine sons, and I'm sorry for it.

Dad

"Here." Boone handed it to Maddie. He didn't trust himself to speak.

Dev rose. "I'm going to leave now, Boone. I don't think I'm needed."

Boone let him go. Asking why would do no good. It was the unanswerable question—why his father didn't realize sooner, before everything went too far. He'd just have to be grateful for what he'd been given.

Boone had Maddie, and that was all that mattered.

The letter was icing on the cake.

He heard her sniff and looked over. Maddie rose and came to stand beside him.

Boone took a seat and pulled her down on his lap, then held on tight. For a long span, they didn't speak, but just held one another.

"He loved you, Boone."

"I guess he did, in his own way."

"Are you angry that he figured it out too late?"

Boone loosened his hold enough to look at her. "I don't know. I can't be angry, because anything changed would mean I might never have met you. If for nothing else, I'll always be grateful to him for that."

"We'll find Mitch. We will," she promised.

He could only nod. He hoped she was right.

"I'm so sad for Sam."

*Such a tender heart.* "He paid a high price." He looked deep into her eyes. "I understand better now. If I lost you—" He wrapped her up tightly in his arms, his voice cracking. "I could be just like him."

Maddie sat up straight and framed his face with her hands. "No, you would never do that. You already showed me that. You were ready to let me go if that's what would make me happy. You're not like him, Boone. You would never make Sam's mistakes.''

''You don't know that.''

Maddie looked deep into his eyes. ''Yes, I do.'' Then she grinned. ''I take it back. You are like him in one way—'' Maddie's eyes twinkled ''—stubborn as sin.''

The weight of the moment vanished with her teasing. ''Anyone ever tell you that you got a mouth on you, Maddie Rose?''

''Why, yes, I believe someone has.''

''I've got better uses for it.'' Boone bent down to show her what he meant.


''You are so beautiful. Rose would have loved to see you in her dress.'' Boone's blue eyes gleamed with tender appreciation.

Maddie nestled against him, loving the moment of quiet they'd stolen on the porch. The entire town of Morning Star, it seemed, was packed inside the big white house that was now her home, having a wedding reception that looked like it might never end.

Boone read her mind. ''Do you think they'll ever leave?'' They'd decided to postpone a honeymoon until the lost siblings had been found.

She smiled. ''Everyone pitched in to make it a dream wedding. They deserve to stay as long as they want. Besides, Vondell's moving into town, and we'll have the place to ourselves soon.''

''Yeah, but you know she'll be around all the time, once you take over The Dinner Bell.'' He chuckled. "It's a long way from a fancy restaurant in New York, Maddie."

"You just wait. I'll have people driving from Fort Worth and Dallas just to eat at my place." Saying the words *my place* sent a surge of pride through Maddie's heart.

"I believe you will," Boone responded, his gaze locking on hers, delivering a deeper layer of meaning. His eyes went dark and hot.

Anticipation tap-danced over Maddie's nerves. For a moment, she couldn't think, lost in the world only she and Boone inhabited.

"If they don't clear out pretty soon, I'm stealing you away, and we're heading for Dallas," he growled. "I've waited too long already to get you naked."

Maddie tried to laugh past the catch in her breath. "Dallas is a long way."

"Forget Dallas. Fifty miles to Brownwood seems like the moon." He tilted her chin up and sealed his mouth to hers in a hungry kiss.

Maddie's knees went weak. She had it all right here—everything she had ever longed for in the years of wandering.

*See if Texas whispers in your heart like it always has in mine.*

*It does, Sam.* In the back of beyond, Maddie had finally found where she belonged.

Then she thought no more, caught up in the magic of the man who had finally let go, finally opened up a wounded heart and let her inside to find a love that still staggered her with its abundance. Maddie answered his kiss with a hunger that matched his.

Suddenly, with breathless ease, Boone swept her up in his arms and strode to the open front door of the house that held everything Maddie had ever dreamed.

"It's almost midnight," he called out. "Everybody clear out of Maddie's house." He grinned down at her, his smile wicked and inviting.

*"Boone's house,"* she corrected. For a woman who'd wanted nothing more than a place of her own a few short weeks ago, it was easy now to relinquish claim. She'd live in a mud hut as long as Boone was there.

*"Our* house," Boone murmured, as he lowered his head to hers. "And *my* woman." He started up the stairs with her, casting one last order over his shoulder.

"Last one out, turn off the lights."

Maddie's giggle turned to a sigh as Boone kissed her.

\* \* \* \* \*

*Be sure to look for
the next book from Jean Brashear.
Don't miss Mitch's story,
coming in February 2000,
only from Silhouette Special Edition.*

If you enjoyed what you just read,
then we've got an offer you can't resist!

# Take 2 bestselling
# love stories FREE!
# Plus get a FREE surprise gift!

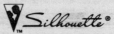

"Fascinating—you'll want to take
this home!"
—Marie Ferrarella

"Each page is filled with a brand-new
surprise."
—Suzanne Brockmann

"Makes reading a new and joyous
experience all over again."
—Tara Taylor Quinn

See what all your favorite authors
are talking about.

*Coming October 1999 to a retail store near you.*

# Sometimes families are made in the most unexpected ways!

Don't miss this heartwarming new series from
**Silhouette Special Edition®, Silhouette Romance®**
and popular author

# DIANA WHITNEY

Every time matchmaking lawyer
Clementine Allister St. Ives brings a couple
together, it's for the children...
and sure to bring romance!

August 1999
**I NOW PRONOUNCE YOU MOM & DAD**
**Silhouette Special Edition #1261**
Ex-lovers Powell Greer and Lydia Farnsworth knew *nothing*
about babies, but Clementine said they needed to learn—fast!

September 1999
**A DAD OF HIS OWN**
**Silhouette Romance #1392**
When Clementine helped little Bobby find his father, Nick Purcell
appeared on the doorstep. Trouble was, Nick wasn't Bobby's dad!

October 1999
**THE FATHERHOOD FACTOR**
**Silhouette Special Edition #1276**
Deirdre O'Connor's temporary assignment from Clementine
involved her handsome new neighbor, Ethan Devlin—and
adorable twin toddlers!

*Available at your favorite retail outlet.*

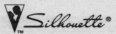